Devour Me

Master Chefs #1

Kailin Gow

Devour Me (Master Chefs Book #1)

Devour Me
Published by Sparklesoup Inc.
Copyright © 2013 Kailin Gow

For information, please contact:

Sparklesoup Inc.
Sparklesoup.com
First Edition.

Kailin Gow

DEDICATION

This dedication is for all women who find men who can cook very sexy :D

Prologue

Taryn Cummings bit her lower lip as an excited thrill shot through her. Her taxi pulled up in front of the building she`d be calling home for the next little while… if all went well.

Here in front of her was the International Institute of Culinary Arts, and her future, her dream of joining the ranks of top chefs.

"Taryn? Are you still there?"

"Oh, Mom," Taryn shouted gleefully into her phone as she pulled a few Euros from her wallet. "Yes! Yes! Oui! Oui! I'm just now arriving at my apartment. I'm so excited, Mom. Paris, can you believe it? This is more than I ever dreamed of."

"I know," Samantha said. "And I'm happy for you, honey."

Taryn heard the strain in her mother's voice. While she knew her mother was indeed happy for her,

4

she also knew she desperately needed a helping hand back home.

"Mom, I won't let you down. When I'm through here, I'm going to come home a great chef and you'll see what I'll do with our little East Side restaurant. I'll turn it into the greatest place in all of New York City. Errol King is the best chef in the world and I hear he's a pretty good teacher, too. I'm going to soak up all the knowledge he has to offer. "

Samantha chuckled. "Yes, I've heard he is quite the teacher."

"Mom, just because the guy is young and good looking doesn't mean he can't be a good teacher."

"No, but it does mean a lot of young and impressionable young female students are going to have a hard time concentrating on cooking… a meal, that is."

Taryn grinned. Chef King was certainly charming. He'd even taken to showing off his charms in a recent print add wearing only his very brief briefs. Fanning her face, Taryn tried to put the heated image aside. "I've seen cute guys before, Mom. I'm here to work and nothing else."

Samantha let out a warm laugh. "That's funny. I could have sworn I saw a few magazines that talked about the handsome young chef along with a lot of interesting photos, too."

The sexy photos of Errol King's muscular tanned body, barely covered by skimpy thong underwear came back to Taryn's mind. "There were some very interesting articles with those photos, Mom."

"Hmm, yes, I'm sure there was. Look, don't worry about the restaurant for now, sweetie. I'll do just fine. You have fun in Paris and call me once you're settled in."

"Oui, oui!" Taryn paid the fare, grabbed her coffee and stepped out of the taxi. "I'll call you tonight."

She slipped her phone into her purse as the taxi driver pulled her bags out of the trunk and set them on the curb. He nodded and mumbled as he made his way back into his cab.

"Thank you," Taryn called out. "Merci!"

As she turned to grab her luggage, a rambunctious chocolate Lab came around the corner and slammed into her. "Oh no!" With her warm and sweet coffee splattered across the front of her dress, she looked at the dog with affectionate reproach. "And why are you in such a hurry?"

The big dog sat and looked woefully at her, his big, dark eyes begging her for forgiveness.

"*Ah, mon Dieu. Javier, mais que fait tu la?*" An older gentleman with a distinguished air about him, came up to Taryn, an empty dog collar hanging from the end of a short leash. "*Milles pardons, Mademoiselle.*"

"I'm sure he didn't mean any harm, sir." Though she understood little French, it was easy to see he was dismayed by his dog's behavior.

"*Mais, il à tout renverser votre café.*" He quickly slipped the collar around the dog's neck then took Taryn by the elbow. "*S'il vous plait. Laissez-moi-vous acheter un bon café chaud.*"

Taryn politely disengaged herself, but the man persisted. He took her by the arm, chattering all the way as he led her to a nearby café.

"*Le moindres que je peut faire c'est de remplacer votre café.*"

7

Frustrated by her inability to understand him and confused by his actions, she struggled to free herself. "I'm sorry, sir, but I don't really understand French very well, but I'm fine. And my bags... my luggage is there on the..."

The gray haired man relented and released her arm, but put his hand to the small of her back and gently pushed her toward the coffee shop. *"Vous aller voir. Ici c'est le meilleur café du quartier."* The man pointed to the waiter.

"Really, sir, I have to get my things into my apartment and I have to register at the Institute. Please... What do you want from me?"

"He just wants to buy you a cup of coffee." The deep, velvety voice behind her sent a thrill down her spine, and her skin felt a distinctly strong male presence close to her. With a bit of a European accent, the voice held a hint of humor.

Taryn turned to face the source and instantly blushed as she faced the gorgeous young man whom that velvety soft voice belong to...a face whose smiles and piercing blue eyes with dark hair gazed at her so many times from all those magazines. In person, he was even more impressive; tall, strong and imposing with broad shoulders and a chest that filled out his tight v-neck black sweater.

He glanced down at her soiled dress and smiled. "I imagine he feels bad for his dog's faux pas."

"Oh." Taryn could think of nothing else to say. As the blush that heated her face intensified, she hoped he'd simply think she was embarrassed by the situation and not flushed by his horribly, terribly, debilitatingly excruciating proximity. He stood so close to her, she could smell him.

Damn, she thought. He even smells good; like a man who worked hard, but took meticulous care of himself. His sultry smile exposed perfectly aligned teeth that gleamed. His dark hair fell in thick curls almost to his shoulders and it wasn't hard to understand how he'd landed the brief brief's ad campaign. Dark, sexy and talented... perhaps even a spark of danger in his eyes; tempting danger.

She was overwhelmed with a sudden need to touch him, to get close to him. The air around her grew suddenly too warm, and her face felt flushed. Without realizing it, she'd leaned in closer to him and when her knees buckled slightly, he quickly took a hold of her arm and held her steady.

"You okay?"

"Yes, I'm fine." She got control of her emotions and straightened up. "I'm sorry. I should have studied a little more French, but…"

Errol looked at the older man. "*Ca va aller, Monsieur. Merci.*"

"*Il n'y a pas de quoi.*" The gentleman nodded at Taryn and turned to speak to a waiter, all while holding his dog leash close to his hip.

"American, I take it." Errol looked pointedly at Taryn.

"Maybe." Taken aback by his question, she looked at him with a slightly defensive scowl. "What of it?"

"Nothing," he said with a chuckle. "I heard you mention you'd be a student at the Institute. It's been a while since an American has studied there. Most students are from Europe, some from Asia and a few from Africa and the Middle East. We barely get a handful of Americans, and they're mostly men."

"Oh." For a moment she wondered if her American status was an asset or a bad disappointment.

"Having an American woman at the Institute is a delightful surprise." Heat smoldered in his gaze as he took her in. "I'm Errol, Errol King." He shook her hand. "I'll be teaching a class this semester."

"Really?" Taryn said, trying to keep the excitement she felt hidden.

The older man returned with a steaming cup of coffee. "Voila."

"Oh, no. You don't have to…"

"You should take that" Errol whispered.

Taryn glanced at the man then back at Errol who nodded.

"This is Dr. Philippe Emanuelle, Head Administrator at the Institute." He turned to the man. "Dr. Philippe, this is a new American student at the Institute, a Mademoiselle…"

"Taryn, Taryn Cummings." She extended her hand to greet the prominent Frenchman. "I'm so pleased to meet you, Doctor." In the far reaches of her mind, a few French words came to her. *"Heureuse de vous connaitre, Docteur."*

11

"I think he wants to make sure you have your dose of caffeine before you get to the Institute."

"Oh." She accepted the cup of coffee. "Thank you. *Merci*."

"After all, the Institute is the toughest culinary school in the world. We churn out the best... we're that good, but we do want to make sure everyone is well prepared to succeed... so, if caffeine is what you need, well, caffeine is what you'll get."

"I appreciate it, but it's not that dire a need." She held the cup up to show the man her appreciation and gently patted the dog on the head.

"Dr. Emmanuelle is very fond of taking Javier for a walk on his break. Every Friday he brings him to school then takes him to the park at the end of the day."

"I can understand why. On the taxi ride over I saw a beautiful park, and it's such a lovely day."

"*A tout a l'heure*." Dr. Emmanuelle nodded and led his dog out of the café.

Errol stepped closer to Taryn, his blue-eyed gaze intense and heated on her. "I suggest you take advantage of this lovely day while you can. Classes can be very challenging and demanding."

"You make it sound so hard. I love to cook and I'm sure I won't have any trouble keeping up."

"A passion for culinary arts is admirable and much needed, but you need more; determination, perseverance... stamina." His gaze went from her eyes to her lips and back up to her eyes. The small glance, as simple as it was, made her lower body clench. Errol held her gaze. "This isn't fun and games. It's serious."

"I fully expect it to be... and I'm very serious about it. I want to come out of this a top chef," Taryn managed to say.

"Good." He licked his lips while his gaze dipped down to the coffee stain at the front of her dress and down to her exposed legs.

The heat was suddenly more than she could handle and she stepped out into the fresh air. The moment she turned around to face him again, the heated intensity of his gaze sent a wave of arousal over every inch of her body. His sapphire eyes seemed to undress her slowly, taking in her every curves. Her clothes seemed inadequate and she felt nude and

13

exposed before him. It made her both thrilled and embarrassed at the same time.

She knew the fabric of her bra was thin, as was the cotton of her dress. In addition to that, the thin cotton of her dress was plastered to the thin fabric of her bra with brown coffee, drawing attention to her erect nipples peeking through her dress. She didn't even dare to look down at the picture she presented him.

Could he see through all that thin fabric and see how aroused she was? Could he see the glow of perspiration on her skin, the sensual flush of her cheeks or the pulpy flesh of her lips?

"You know, you have the kind of passion I like seeing in my students." His gaze trailed over her body again. "I'm sure you'll do fine." He lightly touched his fingertips to her shoulder and leaned in closer.

For a moment she thought he'd kiss her and she didn't know is she should be shocked or elated.

"The first year's tougher than you think. The best way to ace your classes is to pay attention to everything the instructor does, and make sure you know what he or she wants."

14

A few short, sharp breaths escaped her lips before she could speak. "You don't say." She took a step back. "I had kind of planned on that."

Unable to endure his intoxicating presence any longer, she turned to walk away, but he pulled her back. "You have all these bags to bring to your apartment?"

"Yeah, and I'm not really sure which entrance I'm supposed to take."

"I wish I could help you, but…"

She nodded her understanding. "It wouldn't be appropriate…"

"No," he said as he flashed a magnificent smile worthy of a Hollywood close-up. "I guess it wouldn't."

"Right." Taryn snapped out of the daze that had taken over her brain. He was to be her teacher for the next semester and here she was already drooling all over him. She put her hand to the handle of her large suitcase and dreaded lugging it around all alone.

"I'll see you in class." He turned to walk away.

"Mr. King," she blurted out before she could stop herself. "As inappropriate as it may be, I really do need your help. I could walk through this maze of apartments for hours and I have all these bags to…"

"Say no more." With a warm smile that seemed to say so much, he slipped his hand over hers and took her suitcase.

Chapter 1

They walked to the address Taryn had scribbled on a piece of paper, only to realize the address didn't exist.

"I don't understand. I took this down as I spoke to the woman about the apartment. I know my French isn't very good, but I know my numbers."

"Phone connections can sometimes be scratchy. Maybe you misunderstood one of the numbers." Errol took the piece of paper from her hand and looked at the numbers. "Follow me."

Confident he knew the apartment she was looking for, she followed him, but was surprised when he stopped at a dark and expensive looking car.

"We can't spend all day running around in circles," he explained when he caught her gaze. "This'll be much easier."

He popped the trunk open and set her suitcase and bags in it then opened the passenger door.

"I guess it's a good thing you decided to stick around to help me," Taryn said as she slipped into the luxurious leather seat.

When she reached for the seatbelt, Errol took it from her hand. "Here, let me. These can be tricky sometimes." He pulled the seatbelt over her and buckled her in, his knuckles lightly brushing across her breasts, causing her to stop breathing for a second. "There you go. All set." He pulled the buckle tight.

As her gaze travelled over the rich interior and she fought to keep from running her hands over the soft leather, she thought of all the horror stories she'd read about Chef King. He had a notorious reputation for being hard, harsh and uncompromising. On more than one occasion, sous-chefs have left the kitchen in tears. Yet here he was, as charming as could be.

He got into the driver's seat and she took another look at him. Could it be his rough and tough exterior hid a real sweetheart of a man?

"The address you took down is six, four, four, one. My guess is that you mistook a seven for a six."

As he pulled into the street and turned in to opposite direction of the Institute, her heart fell. She'd planned on walking to school every day. If he drove much further and his guess was right… there was no money in her budget for taxis; not even bus fare.

After several blocks he pulled up in front of an old building that appeared rich with history, but poor in luxury.

"This is it."

"The architectural detail is pretty." She looked up at the trimmings on the windows as she got out of the car.

"I like your optimism." Errol got her suitcases out of the trunk and slammed it shut.

A heavy set woman with a scowl permanently etched on her face came out on the front steps and looked critically at the pair then skeptically at the expensive car. "Mademoiselle Cummings?"

"*Oui*," Taryn said, hoping the woman would simply hand her the key to her new abode and not ask a million and one questions.

No such luck. The woman spewed out a torrent of French words that left Taryn staring blankly at her from the curb.

"*C'est tres bien*," Errol said.

The woman disappeared into the building.

"What was all that?"

"Your standard rules. No parties. No loud music. No late payments. She's going to get your key."

"Good. Thanks."

They waited for a moment, a moment that left Taryn terribly aware of all the sensations that coursed through her body. An hour ago she was just another girl from New York trying to find her way in Paris and now she stood shoulder to shoulder with the world's most renown, not to mention the sexiest, chef.

"*Voila.*" The woman handed the keys to Errol and barely glanced at Taryn.

Even at her age, the woman was taken in by Errol's good looks and charm, Taryn thought with a wry grin.

"*Merci.*" Errol affectionately patted the woman's hand as he took the keys, and even offered her a flirtatious wink.

That was enough to turn the permanent scowl into a brief, girlish smile.

With suitcases in hand, they walked up the dingy and dimly lit stairs to the third floor. Errol inserted the key and looked at Taryn. "Ready."

"As I'll ever be."

He opened the door and Taryn gagged.

The tiny, miniscule apartment was as dingy as the stairwell. From where she stood, she could see the entire apartment; the kitchen counter to the right, a half moon dining table pushed up to the wall on the left and a bed set in the middle of it all.

"This is the only place you could find?" Errol asked with unabashed disdain.

"It was the only one I could afford." Tears stung her eyes as a sudden bout of homesickness engulfed her. She took a few uncertain steps into the apartment and gagged again as the odor of mold and mildew assailed her nostrils. Putting her hand over her mouth and nose, she looked down at the bare mattress. It was heavily stained and several springs were painfully visible. "I can't believe…" she muttered.

"This is an abomination. How dare that woman. I wouldn't let a dog sleep here."

His comment did nothing to lighten her mood.

"I have to let some fresh air in here." Taryn headed to the window and pulled the flimsy curtains aside. A large spider, comfortably nestled in folds that had apparently not moved in ages, dropped to the window sill. "Oh, my God." The hysterical scream shot out of her.

In an instant, Errol was at her side and with his bare hand, put an end to the ugly arachnid.

"Oh, that was so gross," Taryn said.

"You're welcome," he shot over his shoulder as he headed to the kitchen sink to wash his hand.

Taryn turned to him when she heard him grumble. "Now what?"

"I don't know which is dirtier; my hand or the water." Rusty colored water drizzled out of the ancient faucet.

Taking a deep breath, Taryn dropped her gaze to the floor as the weight of the world settled nicely on her shoulders. Paris... Glamour, fashion, the Eiffel Tower... and this. She looked outside and wasn't at all surprised when she realized her window faced a stone wall barely four feet away.

A large lump of emotion rose to block her throat. Don't you dare cry, she berated herself. You're from New York, for heaven's sake. Don't you dare cry... especially in front of Errol King.

She unlatched the window and tugged it open. The strong, pungent and nauseating scent of urine quickly entered the room. "Oh, my God." She slammed the window shut.

"This place is unlivable. It should be condemned."

"All the other apartments in this building are rented out, so it is livable. I guess I just need to spend a bit of time sprucing it up."

"Sprucing it up?"

"Yeah." She tried to put some cheer in her voice. "A nice coat of paint; yellow or maybe pink. I could buy some kind of mattress cover and top that with colorful linen."

"Really? And what about the smell?"

"Stores are full of room deodorizers. I'll buy one that smells like vanilla."

"I think you'll have to buy more than one."

Trying to remain optimistic, she ran her hand over the old porcelain kitchen sink, but immediately brought her hand up when her fingers ran through something sticky. "Ew."

"That's enough," Errol said with finality. "No amount of paint, linens and deodorizers is going to make this place livable. We'll have to find you something else."

"Okay," she relented. "Tomorrow, I'll look through the papers and try to find something more suitable, but like I said, my budget doesn't allow for anything more expensive than this."

"Budget or not, you're not staying here." He took a hold of her elbow. "Not even tonight."

"Hey, wait a minute," she said. She freed herself and looked pointedly at him. "I'm not rolling in dough as you apparently are. This isn't something I can just fix with the snap of my fingers. I can't just whip out some gold card and have everything I desire. This is literally all I can afford. I don't even have any money left over to take the bus to get to school."

"All the more reason for you to leave this place." With more determination, he grabbed her arm.

"You really think you can walk this distance to and from school every day? And after the days you'll be spending on your feet sautéing, grilling and roasting? You won't last a week."

"You underestimate me." Though she didn't pull her arm free, she planted her feet to the floor and resisted his tug. "I'm from New York... New York City. Do you know what that means?"

"You think that tough New York grit will be enough to help you survive here? I'll say it again; you won't last a week."

"But..."

"Listen to me. If you're as serious about becoming a chef as you say you are, you'll come with me, because all you'll get from staying here is a failing grade, and maybe diphtheria."

"And where are you planning on bringing me?" An erotic thrill shot through her as the sudden thought of living with him came to mind. No, she quickly corrected herself. He wouldn't do that. He couldn't.

"A place where you can actually inhale." With that he guided her in front of him, picked up her bags and nudged her forward.

In the car, Taryn watched as dingy old buildings turn into immaculate, historic jewels. The sidewalks were wider, the lighting brighter and the view of the Eiffel Tower... Taryn gasped when she saw it.

"It's such an iconic symbol of Paris. I can't believe I'm actually looking at the real thing."

"Get used to it." Errol guided the car into an underground parking lot and led the way to the elevator.

When he opened the door to an apartment, Taryn was immediately face with a spectacular view of the Eiffel Tower. Letting her bags fall to the floor, she rushed to the large windows and looked over Paris.

"But I can't possibly impose myself on you," she said, wishing desperately that he'd argue the point. As inappropriate as it was for her to be there, it was exactly the Paris she'd hoped to experience. The place was breathtakingly beautiful.

"It's no imposition. I'm happy to help out."

She turned to him and wondered what excited her more; being there with him or being in such a fabulous part of Paris. "I'll look for a new place and I'll be out of your hair before you know it."

"There's no rush." He walked to his immaculate kitchen and opened the refrigerator. "Want something to drink?"

"I'll pay you what I was going to pay for the other apartment." On finishing her sentence, she bit her lip. "Well… actually, I had already paid for the other one and I'm going to be a bit low on cash, so…"

"Look, don't worry about all that. I'd rather have you here where you can eat and sleep and work hard in my class than to have you in that cesspool that would no doubt have left you unable to function in class at all." He held up a blue glass bottle. "Water?"

She nodded and accepted the bottle. "Well, that's really nice of you, but I want to do something to repay you. Maybe there's some work I can do around here, you know… tidy up or something."

"I already have someone who takes care of that, but I'll give your offer some thought."

"I feel better if you did." She took a sip of the expensive looking bottled water and was disappointed to find that it simply tasted like any other water she'd ever tasted.

"Less like an intruder?"

"Less of a burden."

"You know, there is something you can do for me."

"Great. What is it? Paperwork? Laundry? Cooking?"

They looked at one another and laughed.

"I think I can handle the cooking," Errol said. "No, Taryn, what I had in mind was something completely different."

Most of her friends called her Taryn and she was often quick to invite new acquaintances to do the same, yet she was certain she hadn't asked Errol to do so. She was caught off guard by how swiftly he'd become familiar with her.

"To tell you the truth," he went on. "I hadn't planned on mentioning it so soon, after all we've just met, but since the opportunity has presented itself..." He set his bottle water on the granite countertop and stepped closer to her. With his eyes intently fixed on hers, he slipped his hands under her jacket and pushed it off her shoulders.

Taryn gulped down a strange combination of arousal and fear. What was he doing?

"I couldn't wait to meet you, Taryn." He wrapped one arm around her waist and delicately fingered her cheek with his free hand.

Her eyes narrowed with suspicion while her body screamed out its desire to be fully satisfied. The strong, warm fingers that played on the small of her back nearly drove her wild, and having his so close...

This can't be, she thought. I'm dreaming. Or is this some freakish nightmare. "How...?" Unable to form any semblance of a question, she simply looked into the deep pools of his blue eyes.

"Your application." He let his answer sink in before going on. "From the very moment I saw your photo, I was intrigued. And when I read your personal essay..." He chuckled, a sound that rumbled with eroticism. "It made me all the more eager to meet you."

Baffled, Taryn stared at him. This man, this sex god who'd starred in more than one erotic dream of hers... he was intrigued... by her? It couldn't be.

"We come from similar backgrounds, Taryn."

Her name had never sounded so sensual and she longed to hear him say it while in the throes of passion.

"I know the area of New York you're from. Just looking at your photo and reading about you, I knew I had to..." He swallowed and narrowed his eyes as his gaze dipped into the opening of her shirt. Licking his lips, he brought his gaze back to her eyes.

Her mouth filled with the need to have him, to taste him. She wanted to lose herself in the depths of his blue eyes and never come up for breath.

"I have to admit, though. The photo didn't do you justice." He reached for a lock of blond hair. "You're even more beautiful in person."

While the girly girl in her was flattered – after all, it wasn't every day she got noticed by a celebrity chef, not to mention one who was so undeniably hot – the strong-willed woman who worked hard to build a promising career was a little miffed.

"Are you telling me you accepted my application based on my looks?"

He cocked a surprised brow. "No, not at all. I was equally impressed by your qualifications. Besides, it's a committee that has the final say, and they are the ones who accepted you... much to my pleasure."

The hand at the small of her back played over her skin, exciting her more than she would have thought possible. When he brought his hand to her waist and gently stroked his thumb just under her breast, she let out a startled gasp.

"You're my teacher," she muttered in mild protest.

"Yes," he said in a deep voice. The hand that had stroked her cheek trailed its way to her lips. "Such beautiful lips," he grumbled. "You can drop my class, you know."

He passed his thumbs over her lower lip and slowly worked his way into the warmth of her mouth.

Without questioning her actions, she sucked on the digit and closed her eyes. She didn't want to drop his class. He was the reason she wanted to go to the Institute. She wanted to learn everything she could

31

from him. She wanted to know him, get closer to him...sucking on his finger only made her want to explore more of him. "No, I want you..." she barely whispered. Shocked by her own admission she was going to stop sucking on his finger when he pulled out and begin tracing her lips with it so softly and sensuously, it felt like a kiss.

"I knew I'd find pleasure behind the innocent pout to these sultry lips." He leaned in to kiss her and his tongue received the same treatment his thumb had. Her mouth latched on, devouring his tongue with the passion she had harbored for him, after all those years of having a celebrity crush on him.

He kissed her back passionately, his tongue entwining in hers, stroking her mouth until she shuddered against him. "What I'd questioned was the response of your body." That said, he passed the thumb that'd stroked beneath her breast over her nipple.

The response was swift.

"Yes," he whispered into her ear as his thumb worked around the erect nipple. "You liked being touched, don't you, Taryn."

Her answer came in the way of a sensually charged groan. Though the thin fabric of her bra allowed for a wonderful sensation, she longed to feel his fingers against her skin.

He cupped her breast. "I noticed it in your eyes the moment I saw you. You're spirited and independent, but you respect authority and are accustomed to doing as you're told. That makes for a good student, but it also makes for a good..." He pressed the hardness of his erection against her. After a brief, but thrilling gasp from Taryn, he pulled back.

In the back of her mind, she knew she had an argument to make, but her body refused her that luxury. It was fully enthralled by the working of his hand over her breast, urging it to delve under the fabric of her bra with every subtle arching of her back.

"You enjoy pleasing people, don't you, Taryn." His lips left her ear and travelled down the length of her neck. "And I enjoy being pleased."

She struggled to find her voice. She had to say something, anything to make him understand this wasn't what she'd expected. In her wildest dreams, yes, but in reality...she had her scholarship to think of.

"What...?" The question remained lodged in her throat as he brought his lips into the valley between her breasts.

"You and I will get along quite well." He brushed his hardened erection against her, making her shudder with need for him. She had never been touched so boldly by a man.

"Wait." Through her lustful daze, Taryn found the strength to stop him. "I have no intention of prostituting myself in order to have a nice place to live or to get good grades."

"That's not my intention either."

"Really? Then why are your hands and lips all over me?"

A pleased chuckled purred through his parted lips while his eyes danced with amusement. He took his hands off her and took a step back making her instantly regret her words. Her body now felt cold and alone without the warmth of his closeness.

"I'm happy to see you find this all amusing," she managed to say. "But I have my future at stake here. What will people think when they learn I'm living with my teacher."

"What I have in mind is completely legitimate and people will think you're damned lucky."

Taryn cocked an intrigued brow. "Go on."

"I need a live-in assistant and have made no secret about it. I'm in the process of writing a new cookbook and I need someone to try out the recipes. It's a lot of work, work I don't have time to tend to. I'm already swamped. Between teaching, taping my show and the publicity tours, I barely have time to take a breath. And I'm already behind my deadline. Of course, I need someone with a strong culinary background. You'd have to write down every change, every adjustment, edit everything, organize everything."

A little confused by the sexually charged reception and the now cool calculation of his arrangement, Taryn shrugged off the vague disappointment that'd settled on her shoulders and concentrated on the positive aspect of this plan. Working for someone as illustrious as Errol King was a definite plus in any résumé.

"I think you're the perfect candidate, Taryn. Do you think it's something you could handle? Something you'd enjoy?"

"I do."

"Then, you accept?"

"Yes, I accept."

"Fantastic. I know you're going to do a great job. Now let me show you to your room."

She followed him into the hall, gawking at her beautiful surroundings. Living in such an apartment was a dream. And when he pushed the door to her room open she knew it was a dream she could easily get used to.

Elegantly furnished and tastefully decorated, the room immediately embraced her. The neutral colors were warm and inviting, as was the throw rug by the bed. Large throw cushions on the bed added the only splash of color in the room; a deeply burnt orange and a blood red.

"Think you'll be comfortable here?"

"I might never want to leave." She walked to the window, certain the view behind the curtain would be better than the one she would have had were it not for his generous invitation. She wasn't disappointed. "And I get to wake up to the Eiffel Tower every morning."

"It's a major part of the reason I chose this location. Isn't it fabulous?"

It's more than fabulous, she thought, feeling more like a princess than in any of her childhood dreams. As she looked out at the city she would call home for the next little while, she heard Errol come up behind her. Her breath caught in her throat when his strong arms wrapped around her waist and pulled her back to his chest.

"I'm glad you decided to come stay here," he said. His lips brushed along her ear. "I was looking forward to seeing you in class, but I guess we were meant to meet earlier. I hope everything will work out well...and if you are very good, in time I might do more to you than touch you, Taryn. I might just bend you over, tear off your panties, and fuck you until you're raw and screaming from having orgasms after orgasms." He nibbled her lobe. "Or devour your delicious puss all day long. You'd like that, wouldn't you?" His fingers snaked their way under her shirt and lightly brushed her breast. "I know I'm already looking forward to it."

For a moment she thought she'd misheard him. Surely she'd misheard... misunderstood. When his hard-on pressed into her backside she realized she'd heard exactly what he'd said and knew exactly what he meant.

New to the strange sensations he continued to bring her since their encounter, she didn't know whether to fight him off or lean into his embrace. It felt good, that much she couldn't deny, but it didn't feel right.

He was a handsome and obscenely rich celebrity, and Taryn knew how many women wished they could be in the very same spot she now found herself in.

And this handsome and obscenely rich celebrity could be my first, she thought. Her first... What would he think when he learned she was a naïve, inexperienced twenty-one year old virgin? He who had probably known hundreds of women; women who knew... who knew what? How to make love to a man? How to touch a man?

How hard could it be?

Biting her lip she looked down at his hands. How many breasts had they cupped? And as his lips continued to play along her neck she wondered how many lips had he kissed. How many women had pleased him?

Did it matter? she thought as he gripped her hips and pulled her back into him, pressing his hard-on more urgently into her backside. She let out an involuntary moan. He was the man of her dreams…now she could have him, and he wanted her, too…

She'd come to Paris to get an education, to build a career and she had every intention of proving herself…to Errol, to Paris, to the culinary world. She had no intention of simply being a man's plaything. She had to do well at the Institute, learn everything she could, and go back home to run her mother's restaurant. Her mother gave up her chance to date and get remarried for her and her little brother. Now it was Taryn's turn to give up her dreams to save the family restaurant and take care of her family. Once she returned to New York, once her time at the Institute was over, she'd go straight to work as hard as her mother at the restaurant and probably never have time for herself.

Taryn's thoughts were interrupted by Errol, and she soon became lost in the pleasure he was giving her. Oh God, his touch felt so good. He smelled good, and whatever he was doing to her, it consumed her, made her whole body and mind respond to him and chased away any other thoughts, except having more of him. He turned her around and pressed his hard-on against her sensitive core and rubbed against her, while his fingers played with her nipples, squeezing them and then circling them. "Errol…" she began to say, but his mouth pressed into hers, his tongue seeking out her tongue. Her head swam in pleasure, while her body took over with desire for him. *It's time to put the little girl behind. It's time to stop turning guys away. It's time to see what all the fuss is about. Why couldn't I enjoy this just one time before I give up my own dreams and a chance for my own life?*

"What do you want, Taryn?" Errol mumbled between kisses.

"I want," she let out. "I want this arrangement, Errol," she confessed. For the first time in her life she was ready to jump into a meaningless and purely physical relationship with a man… and who better than Errol King?

Chapter 2

Just as Taryn prepared to lean back and give in, Errol backed away, released her and headed to the bedroom door.

"I know you've had a big day, so I'll let you get settled. If you want to do some shopping tomorrow – buy a few things you might have forgotten – I'd be happy to take you to a few shops. We can also stock the refrigerator with whatever you like."

Chilled by his sudden turn toward the pragmatic, Taryn hugged herself, willing the chill to leave her. She wanted his arms again and couldn't understand how he could be so hot and passionate one moment then turn around and treat her as though she were a mere houseguest.

You are a mere houseguest, she reminded herself.

"Thank you," was all she could say as she followed him out.

"I have to get to the Institute. I'll see you later." Without so much as a peck on the forehead, he left.

Though dismayed, Taryn's spirits soared as she reminded herself where she was… in the heart of Paris. Letting out a childish yelp, she spun around in the living room, ran to the kitchen to check out the contents of each cupboard then ran to Errol's room to see what the room said about him.

Rich with fine antiques, his room was a blend of refinement and masculinity. Several authentic looking masterpieces hung on the walls in intricately carved picture frames. A curio case in the far corner held a surprising variety of knick knacks, most notably a porcelain figurine of a small boy kicking a ball while being chased by his dog. It seemed strangely innocent and charming in the otherwise mature décor.

Running her hand over the bed, she immediately felt a spark and knew it was a spark borne of Errol's touch on her skin. Why had he not continued his sensual onslaught on her and invite her to share his large bed? She had been so aroused by him, she wanted him to take her then and there. Why did he stopped?

"No," she said aloud to the darkened walls that had probably seen their fair share of wanton acts in this room. "I will not spend the day wallowing in angst because some hotheaded chef doesn't want to go to bed with me."

She marched out and spent the better part of the morning organizing her things. Her dresses, skirts and blouses fit neatly in the oversized closet while the dresser drawer remained half empty even after she'd unpacked her last suitcase.

With her bedroom in order, she made her way to the kitchen carrying a small cardboard box. Inside were the few cooking implements she couldn't live without. A Lamson perforated turner she treated herself to the previous year, a wooden spoon her mother had given her after they'd concocted their first sauce together, a professional Japanese knife from Chroma France she'd won when she'd entered a Eurasian cooking contest and her favorite pepper mill from Peugeot; a birthday gift from her brother, Bobby. As a young college student, he'd had to work many hours in order to set aside enough money for the tool he'd call, 'a waste of a good fifty bucks.'

She opened the drawer to put the turner, spoon and knife away, wondering what Errol would say when he found them. No doubt he would balk at the wooden spoon and call it an unprofessional utensil. Chuckling as she anticipated his return, she set the pepper mill on the counter.

As the lunch hour approached, she decided to whip up a light lunch for Errol. A fresh summer salad, some French bread with melted Brie and confit onions, and rolled caramels in a warm vanilla custard for dessert.

Working in Errol's kitchen was a dream. Functional, practical, convenient and modern, it had everything a chef needed to prepare meals and even a few things she would have never thought of, like the vegetable rinsing basket incorporated into the sink and a superimposed glass counter that stood eight inches above the main countertop. It allowed one to work on the main countertop while keeping certain items close and handy on the glass shelf.

The entire kitchen was a far stretch from the small and sometimes confusing kitchen she'd work in back home. As cramped and untidy as it was, however, it never diminished her love of cooking.

Cooking had always pleased her, always brought out the triumphant child in her, and even preparing a light and simple lunch brought her pleasure. The colors, textures, scents and flavors had always enticed her, called out the creator in her, and she always responded. It had always been with her; not only the love of good food, but the pleasure of feeding those around her. Her friends and family had benefited from that passion on more than one occasion.

Now it was Errol's turn.

An hour and a half after preparing the quick lunch, however, she realized he would not be coming back. Half-heartedly, she ate her meal and wondered if he'd be home for dinner.

He wasn't, and arrived only shortly before she prepared for bed.

"Oh, you're still up." With an overstuffed folder tucked haphazardly under his arm, he brushed past her and headed to the kitchen.

"It's been a long day, but I had time to get cozy and feel at home here."

"I'm happy to hear that." He opened the refrigerator and pulled out a bottle of water. "Don't let me keep you up. Tomorrow I'll have a few hours free so I can show you some of the best places to shop, if you like."

"Um, yeah. Sure, that'd be great." Had she really heard a dismissal in there somewhere? While she'd hardly expected him to jump all over her when he arrived, she had expected something... a little warmth. Okay, she silently admitted. She had expected him to jump all over her. So why the coldness?

She went to bed, confused. Did she imagined this sensual man's touch on her earlier today? She sighed. It must have been real, but she was too exhausted to think otherwise, and she fell asleep.

The following morning he awaited her bright and early in the kitchen with a steaming cup of strong coffee.

"I thought we'd start with a tour of the local markets. I have my favorite spots – the freshest bread, the best beef, the crispest vegetables – but you can decide for yourself where you eventually want to shop."

Taryn barely had time to gulp down a few sips of coffee and get dressed before they headed out in search of the perfect ingredients for the day's meals.

The fish market produced the perfect halibut steak for dinner while various vegetable vendors provided the carrots, onions and spinach that would accompany it. They picked out a lean cut of beef that would be thrown into a fresh Mediterranean salad with pearl onions and olives. Fresh baked bread called to them from a distance as the heavenly scent wafted through the tightly packed streets and Errol treated her to a warm and gooey brioche straight from the oven of his favorite baker.

"Think you'll remember where all of these are?" He gestured at the many vendors as they continued to wind their way through the marketplace.

Taryn licked her fingers as she finished her last bite. "Sure. Everything is pretty much in the same area."

"Don't get lost. I told my editor I finally found someone to test my recipes; I can't afford to lose you now."

His statement was pure business and held no trace of the erotic proposition he'd made the night before.

"When do you want me to get started?" She hoped she sounded as businesslike as he did.

"I'll give you a few more days to get settled, to get accustomed to your surroundings. I'll be busy at the Institute, preparing for the upcoming classes – which start Monday, by the way. I want to give you a chance to come down here by yourself, test out the produce, maybe make a few meals on your own to get to know my kitchen."

"Which is really fabulous, by the way."

"I wouldn't have it any other way." He entered a small, dark store. "What is a great meal without a great bottle of wine?"

The long, narrow store had floor to ceiling bottles neatly tucked away into hundreds of cubby holes. As if knowing the place by heart, Errol pulled a bottle out.   "Chateau Pepusque of the Languedoc

49

region. One of my favorites. The 2007 is exquisite; the flavor is well-rounded and full. I think you'll enjoy it."

"I'll have to trust you on that. I hardly know anything about wines. I know white goes with fish and red with beef, but other than that…"

He waved the bottle at the owner, who duly jotted down the purchase. "That school of thought has long been followed my many wine drinkers," he said as he led the way out, "but the rules of the game have changed. There are some wonderful juicy reds that can accompany fish, while some whites are perfect for certain cuts of beef."

Their arms laden with packages and bags, they returned to his apartment. They spent the morning preparing a more elaborate lunch than Taryn had prepared the day before. Shoulder to shoulder with such a master, Taryn was even more impressed with his talent.

He minced onions in a flash, crushed a few garlic cloves and diced carrots, a red pepper and some celery.

"Learned anything yet?" He flashed her a proud grin as he sautéed the onions.

"I think I'm holding my own so far." Busy whipping a salad dressing to creamy perfection, she glanced at him and smiled.

They brought their meal out to the sun-filled terrace. Like a true gentleman, Errol pulled a chair out for her and gently pushed the chair in. He poured them each a glass of wine before taking his seat.

"A toast," he said with his glass in the air. "To a profitable, successful and delicious relationship."

Tapping her glass to his, she noted the absence of words like passionate, erotic or sensual. Had his come-ons simply been a way of flirting with her? Or had she imagined it all?

"I read in your résumé that you didn't go to college."

"Money was a bit tight and Mom needed a hand down at the restaurant."

"Are those the reasons or the excuses?"

She laughed. "A bit of both, I guess. I've never been academically talented. You have no idea how arduous it was getting through English classes; all that mumbo-jumbo about objects and verbs and proper nouns, not to mention prepositions and pronouns. Math wasn't so bad, so, yes, I can split a recipe in two or double a recipe without messing it up. Science was so-so and history had a few interesting moments, but not enough to warrant me a grade I can boast about. All in all, I really wasn't the best student, no matter how hard I tried."

"Should I be concerned?" He cocked a mocking brow.

"This isn't the same thing. I'm hungry to learn everything about cooking. I promised my mom I'd turn our little family restaurant into a four-star gem. Instead of just offering deli food and a hodgepodge of international dishes, I want to serve gourmet French cuisine. That's why I'm so eager to learn everything I can here. This is everything high school never even touched on. You know, it's one thing to have to sit and try to absorb what others tell you you should know, and quite another to have the desire to know everything about a subject that interests you. My brother is the complete opposite. He can't get enough of learning about anything and everything. He's eighteen and in college, and he has that endless curiosity that keeps him wanting to learn more. If it were up to him, he'd be a lifelong student."

"You come from a big family?"

"No. Just the one baby brother... Bobby, though he hates it when I call him my baby brother. He considers himself the family protector."

"Protecting you from big, bad men who would take advantage of you?" A hint of teasing playfulness came to his eyes.

"Not only me," she said matter-of-factly. "He's always checking in on my Mom and he guards her parents, my grandparents, with his life."

"I take it your father isn't around."

"You take it right. I never really knew my father. He stuck around long enough to conceive Bobby and he was there, on and off, after he was born, but then he disappeared... something about another calling." She rolled her eyes and waved her hand to indicate she no longer wanted to talk about him. "What about you? I think I read somewhere that you had family here in France."

He nodded heavily. "Nana. Ninety-seven and still kicking butt."

"Are your parents back in the States?"

He snickered and waved his fork around. "They're probably off with your father somewhere."

"Oh," she murmured. "Sorry to hear that." She'd read that his grandmother was immensely important to him and that she'd had a hand in raising him, but had never known what had happened to his parents. Somewhere in the fantasy of it all, she'd imagined they'd had an accident and died. It was troubling to consider they'd abandoned him.

"Don't be. If my parents had no desire to stick around to raise a kid, I was probably better off without them. Besides, I think Nana did a pretty good job raising me."

"Did she influence your love of cooking?"

"Influence? She is single-handedly responsible for where I am today. She seemed intent on turning me into a culinary genius. When I was six, she taught me how to make a perfect omelet. At eight I was already surprising her with my own take on a *croquet-monsieur*. For her eightieth birthday I prepared the

54

entire menu for the whole party – forty-five guests; *hors-d'oeuvres, pot-au-feu, crème brulée."*

"Hold on," Taryn said as she put her hand up. "You did all this for her eightieth birthday?"

He nodded. "Planned, prepared and helped with the service."

"You're twenty-seven."

A curious frown furrowed his brow. "Yeah?"

"You said your grandmother is ninety-seven."

"Yeah."

She looked up to the sky and pointed her finger in the air as she counted. "That would mean you were only ten years old when she turned eighty."

"I told you… she wanted to turn me into a culinary genius."

"You mean to tell me that you prepared a whole menu, for forty-five people at only ten years old? Come on. I'm naïve, but…"

"Okay, the truth?"

"Come clean," she dared.

"The butcher helped by pre-cutting all the pieces of meat I needed for the *pot-au-feu*. Nana always gave me plenty of freedom, but working with

55

large, sharp knives when I was alone was a definite no-no. I was able to manage the dicing of the vegetables on my own though. Nana did give me a helping hand with the crème brulée."

"And a chef was born."

"I have to admit I'd been bitten by the cooking bug. Everyone there gushed over the quality of the meal and I knew I wanted to feel that sense of victory again."

Taryn looked at him and noticed for the first time the man he really was. She'd heard so much talk about him… how tough and brutal he could be, how unforgiving. Many rumors circulated about the number of sous-chefs he'd fired, all for minor offenses.

But as she looked at him now, she saw the little boy who'd found a passion thanks to the loving hand of a sweet old woman he called Nana. Maybe he wasn't so bad after all. Maybe he was just one of those horribly misunderstood celebrities.

She looked into his brilliant blue eyes, eyes made all the more intense by the dark waves of hair that framed his face. As much as she enjoyed the thought of ending up in his bed, she was pleased with this side of him. Maybe it was for the best.

Chapter 3

The week continued with the same leisurely and casual pace as that quiet and intimate lunch. Taryn and Errol discovered each others' little quirks, their strange idiosyncrasies and one or two neurosis.

Errol had an almost military discipline when it came to keeping his kitchen clean. No sooner was a dish no longer needed that it was cleaned, dried and put away. Taryn tended to leave things lying around until her space was a tad crowded then she would rush to clean everything at once, something Errol told her to correct.

"I know," she had said. "Clean as you go. My mom has told me often enough."

Errol counted out every chop as he cut any vegetable, while Taryn always chimed *one potato, two potato*.

As they worked on a variation of a gazpacho, Taryn leaned against the counter and looked at Errol. "What's your take on molecular cooking?"

"A silly, modern trend."

"Did you ever try it?"

"No, but I've tasted the results of a few who have. Either they didn't have the technique down or the desired result was not what I want when I sit down to a meal."

"So, I guess then that we won't be touching on that in class."

"Not in my class." He threw three zucchinis into a food processor and pressed the button until they were pureed.

"Tomorrow, right?"

"Yep. You ready?"

"I've been ready for the past week. I've been ready from the very moment I learned I'd been accepted here."

"You know, the Institute must have seen real talent in you. Few applicants are accepted."

"I know," she gushed.

The next day, Taryn sat front and center in the class of eighteen.

"Today," Errol said after everyone had introduced themselves to the class, "we're going to start with a basic run through of different cuts of beef; which cuts to use in soups, which to grill, and which to roast."

With the help of a PowerPoint presentation, he showed the class the various cuts and gave examples of the best ways to prepare each.

"When preparing a sauce to accompany this cut, what base can you start with?" Errol asked.

"A roux," Taryn said as she shot her hand into the air.

"Interesting, Taryn.... And how would you prepare your roux?"

"I heat up a saucepan and melt a few tablespoons of butter then add the same amount of flour. Then it's just a matter of adding a sufficient amount of liquid, like a really strong tea."

He nodded his acceptance of her answer. "How many of you have attempted to string up a top blade chuck roast?"

A few students tentatively raised their hands, including Taryn.

"How many of you have prepared a rack of lamb?"

Again a few tentative hands rose.

"Okay, so I'm going to have you guys pair up. We're going to put a few quick skills to the test."

Taryn turned to the fair haired young man beside her. His eyes lit up when he noticed she was looking his way.

"Henri, right?" she said as she remembered his introduction.

"Oui," he said. "Yes. We work together, no? Umm... Taryn."

She instantly fell in love with his French accent and his charming manner. Though she estimated he was a year or two younger than her, he seemed strong and capable. "That'd be great, and you can call me Taryn."

"Very good, Taryn. You have *la passion* for *cuisine* like me," Henri said as the remainder of the students tried to find suitable companions.

"I can't imagine myself doing anything else."

"Just like me. I come from a small town. A bit far from *Paris*. I think my father would have preferred I stay on the farm and tend to his herd of cows. Thankfully my mother had bigger plans for me."

"I hope your father wasn't too upset."

"He wanted me to stay, but I think, deep down, he's happy for me."

The class finally settled down and Errol shouted out a series of demands, all to be precisely executed within the shortest amount of time. Several students seemed completely befuddled by the string of requests, while others cursed at their inability to execute properly.

"A *mirepoix*," Errol called out.

Taryn grabbed a handful of carrots and celery while Henri reached for the onion. They chopped madly for sixty seconds then tossed everything into a hot saucepan.

Grinning, they silently congratulated one another. They finished every task first while one other pair was often a close second. On more than one occasion, Taryn caught their glare of open disdain.

"I don't think they like us," Henri noted as Errol barked out another order.

Taryn began trimming the cut of beef they'd been assigned. "I didn't come here to be liked," she said with a shrug.

"I think I'm going to like working with you," Henri said with a playful grin.

"Good," she said. "I like working with you, too."

"Tomorrow we'll take a look at haute cuisine terminology." Errols words sounded unusually harsh. "I thought we could by-pass that, but seeing the looks on your faces when I mentioned a few terms today, I've reconsidered."

Chapter 4

Errol watched Taryn and Henri with keen interest. While he tried to make it look like it was their work he scrutinized, he became aware of staring at Taryn on more than one occasion and quickly averted his gaze.

Her skilled hands impressed him, working with surprising dexterity and speedy precision, but it was the warm and engaging smile she offered Henri that continually caught his attention, stirring something hot and possessive in him.

As soon as they'd paired up, Errol had mentally gone through the young man's résumé. From the region of Pays de la Loire, Henri Boisjoli was the son of a dairy farmer... hardly competition for a top chef.

Forcing himself to scan the room, he nonetheless brought a fleeting glance back to Taryn before continuing his scan. Every pair of students cleaned up their stations and prepared to leave. When he heard Taryn laugh, he turned to her and was surprised to see Henri, the innocent young man from the country, brushing a wisp of long blond hair off Taryn's face.

Affection already gleamed in the young man's eyes.

As the students waved goodbye and filed out of the class, Errol couldn't help but wonder how much time Taryn would spend with the boy. Was she going to her next class with him? Would they have lunch? Dinner?

He shoved the speculation and questions aside until he arrived home later that night. As he pushed the key into the lock he wondered if she'd be there. Perhaps Henri had invited her out for a drink, or a bite to eat.

Did he care? Really? She was just a... He inhaled deeply and reminded himself who he was. He could have any woman. Yes... but he wanted this one. He desired this one.

On opening the door he was flooded with an unusual wave of relief as he heard Taryn humming in the kitchen.

"Don't look," she called out with childish glee. "I'm trying something new."

"Well, it certainly smells good."

"I hope you didn't eat yet."

"Of course not. It's only six-thirty."

"I went to the wine store you brought me to," she said as she emerged from the kitchen and met him in the living area. She offered him a glass of red wine. "I thought you might like this one; *Chateau du Pape..*"

He took a sip, rolled it around in his mouth a moment then swallowed. "A very good choice. And what will you be serving with it?" He looked her over, taking in her casual and relaxed attire that suited her to perfection.

At the institute, students were asked to wear a white chef's jacket to every class; an overcoat that hid any attribution a young woman might have. It pleasured him to now see Taryn in snug yoga pants and a teal tank top that hugged her breasts in a full, well-rounded manner. Her long blond hair was pulled off her face in a neat ponytail. Without a trace of make-up, her face was the picture of clean, fresh beauty. She was breathtaking, a natural beauty, who didn't seem to know how gorgeous she was.

"I had an idea for a hot and spicy take on a rack of lamb," she called over her shoulder as she returned to the kitchen.

"Are my classes already inspiring you?" He absent-mindedly rolled the wine around in the glass while his eyes remained steadfastly on her exiting buttocks…perfectly round, soft, and tight. He felt his jeans tightening in front as he imagined running his hands over them, grabbing them and holding them while he rammed hard into her.

"Actually it's Henri who gave me the idea… you know, the guy I paired up with."

Errol frowned and set the glass of wine on the table. With an unhappy pout pursing his lips, he cracked his knuckles.

"You know, he first gives the impression of being some country bumpkin who doesn't know squat about *haute cuisine*, or any *cuisine* for that matter, but, when you take a minute to talk to him, he really knows what he's talking about."

"That's nice," Errol muttered.

"Dinner should be ready in fifteen minutes."

"I'll hop into the shower then."

"Perfect."

Under the hot running water, Errol tried to scrub off the uneasy sense of insecurity that engulfed him.

He closed his eyes and imagined her, nude, her firm breasts glowing under thick, creamy lather. Droplets trickled down to her navel and onward between her thighs. A thin line of fine blond hair indicated the heated passage he longed to lose himself in.

There was something fiery about her; something hidden behind the innocent, wide eyes. He'd seen it in her frown when he'd released her that first night; the wanting; the desire. Her delicious lips had remained parted in hunger long after he'd left her side.

As he lathered his torso, his hand brushed against the hard-on that cried out for release. Tempted to take a firm grip, to envision Taryn's body against his as he pumped out his need to touch her again, he reached for the faucet and cooled the water.

When his body had thoroughly chilled, he shut the water and patted himself dry. As he returned to his room to dress, he debated whether to dress like the professional he was or to entice Taryn with something more alluring; snug but casual sweatpants that hung low on his hips.

Enticement won.

He looked at his nude torso and imagined her lips on his skin, her tongue licking every ridge of his stomach and while heading down to take him into her mouth. His penis hardened thinking how she would first suck shyly and then hard, vigorously, running her teeth over his sensitive tip. "God, I want you bad," he groaned as he pulled a tight white t-shirt over his head. "I've waited long enough."

"Perfect timing," Taryn exclaimed as he entered the dining room.

The table was beautifully set. The silver candelabra his grandmother had given him; the one he had never used, now sat in the center of the table with three long tapered candles that glowed with romantic promise. His finest china was laid out, as was his flatware.

"If your meal is as good as this table looks, I think I'm going to enjoy having you in my home even more." He narrowed his eyes appreciatively at her blushing cheeks and flushed chest.

"I was afraid you might not take too well to my cooking my own dishes." She sat down facing him then looked down at herself. "Oh, I forgot to change. This is such an elegant meal, I can't just…"

"You look perfect. I like this laid back look."

"Well, in that case." She raised her glass. "*Bon appetit.*"

"*Bon appetit.*"

Taryn looked apprehensively at him as he sliced through the lamb and took his first might.

"The verdict?" she said when he remained silent.

He cocked an impressed brow. "Interesting. Is that cumin I taste?"

"It is."

"And a hint of… what is that?" He took another bite. "Cinnamon?"

"Could be," she said with a pleased and teasing grin.

"It's not something I would have ever thought to try, but… it works. Congratulations."

"I'm happy you like it."

Throughout dinner, they spoke of the upcoming classes and the cookbook that she'd be working on. While he managed to speak clearly enough about his culinary intentions, his mind was far from the kitchen. Repeatedly, his gaze dipped into the valley of her breasts and he was mesmerized by the thought of seeing her completely nude, feeling her soft heated skin against his, her wet folds touching his hardness like a kiss. She'd be as sweet as she looked, but with a touch of spice that seemed to heat up every part of his body. The combination of innocent and sexy was intoxicating to him, especially the hint of defiance in her eyes. He wasn't sure if she despised him, but was humoring him to get ahead. Whatever it was, he wanted to possess her, own her, make her his. His erection harden just thinking about having her naked in his bed, while his mouth worked on her most delicious core. Errol's face darkened with desire as he stared heatedly at her. *He would be damned if he didn't fuck her tonight.*

When she picked up a bone and ravenously sucked on the tip, he nearly dropped his glass of wine. Her lips, perfectly puckered, perfectly sensuous, perfectly set to take him in and... Oh, how delicious it would be.

As wonderful as the meal was, he set his fork down and leaned back with his glass of wine and watched her. One by one, she took each of the four bones on her plate and cleaned them off, picking daintily at the remaining meat with her long slender fingers before sucking the juices off.

He tried to catch her gaze. Did she have any idea the effect she had on him? For all appearances, she seemed oblivious. Her appetite was reserved to the food on her plate and not the hungry man sitting in front of her.

She set her fork down and looked at him. "Without wanting to sound pretentious, I have to admit I impress myself."

"And with good reason. It was a bold move, but the contradiction of flavors was perfectly balanced." He reached out to take her hand. "Looks like I made the right choice it taking you on to test my recipes. You won't have any trouble finding flaws or miscalculations. You'll probably even improve many of them."

She cocked a brow. "Will I get credit?"

"Sure, why not?"

"Really? I was being facetious."

"I might be a pretentious and arrogant bastard when I need to be, but I know how to give credit where credit is due. I might even include this very meal in my book… if that's okay with you."

"Okay? It's more than okay. It's fabulous. Wait until I tell my mother. My own recipe, my own creation in a book as prestigious as yours."

His hand remained over hers and he was dismayed by the lack of physical reaction from her. She didn't grip his fingers or show any sign of welcoming more of his touch. Cool and aloof, she pulled away, stood and cleared the dishes. Did she not have any desire for him?

"Wait until you see what I concocted for dessert."

She returned a minute later. "These are caramelized tangerine slices on a bed of a secret crunchy cereal mix, drizzled with a buttery citrus *coulis*."

"Humm," he mumbled as he chewed on his first bite. "An interesting touch of saltiness that embraces that tartness of the tangerine. Excellent."

Errol was genuinely impressed by the creative boldness of the young woman in front of him so much so that he finished off the evening sitting back and enjoying Taryn's culinary creations, relegating his sexual urges to another day.

Taryn's lack of response tonight puzzled him, yet frustrated him. He was ready to show this innocent beauty all the pleasures her body could take, but instead, her passion was for the culinary dishes she created tonight. He was proud of her bold choices, but frustrated. He didn't want a woman in his bed, who did not want to be there. Yet, he was so certain, she wanted him as badly as he wanted her.

*****

The weeks' classes were a blur of knife skills, storing methods and the preparation of dough and

74

sauces. Every day, Errol was surprised and impressed by Taryn's keen palate and her ability to see what few students saw. She was focused on her studies, and as serious as the most promising students already working professionally at prestigious restaurants were.

Her questions were always straight to the point and her answers articulate.

But what caught his attention was the simple beauty she brought to his class every day. He couldn't take his eyes off of her, nor could he help wanting to get close to her and touch her when he could. While many of the other young female students, and even a few males, tried desperately to gain his attention, his eyes constantly returned to Taryn who continued living under his roof, so close yet so far away. Her sudden indifference to him frustrated him, yet he bid his time. He savored the challenge she posed, knowing when the time came for him to make her his, it would be worth it.

More often than not, her eyes were on Henri, smiling, affectionate and kind. She often helped him where he fumbled, but Errol had to admit, the young man from the countryside had talent, if not a certain boyish charm.

The two together were a powerful force; something that had not gone unnoticed by the rest of the class. It was also clear to any man, the boy was besotted with Taryn, sneaking glances are her when she wasn't looking, finding any excuse to touch her hand or shoulders. Had not Taryn responded so strongly to him that first day they met, Errol would have been concerned about the innocent flirtations Henri shared with Taryn. But Errol, nevertheless, kept his eye on him. And Taryn. Always on Taryn.

Chapter 5

"I loved your class today," Taryn said as she leaned into the counter to watch him clean the oysters, mussels and clams he'd just brought home.

"Really? It was just a revision of what we looked at last week. I was surprised to see the number of students who couldn't handle skinning and filleting a salmon."

"You'll think I'm childish and petty, but I think that's part of the reason I liked it. So many students have been mean and nasty to me. It was kind of nice watching them stumble their way around that poor fish."

Grinning, Errol looked at her. Childish innocence hung around her like a golden aura. It wasn't hard to see why so many of the girls in class disliked her. She was beautiful, smart and talented. As for the boys in the class, obviously Taryn hadn't noticed the way they always looked at her, sneaking a peek whenever she wasn't looking.

Without her even noticing, her rear end always seemed to attract a large amount of that attention from the men. Every time she took her overcoat off at the end of the class, male eyes turned her way. She had an exquisite way of filling out the snug jeans she always wore in class.

"Is it true what they say about oysters?" Taryn asked.

"I don't know. What do they say about oysters?"

Taryn shot him a quirky smirk. "You're a chef. You were raised in France. You're reported to be a sex machine. Don't try to tell me you don't know what everybody else says about oysters. I'm sure even your Nana knows."

"Oh, the sex thing." He held up a perfect specimen. "These?"

"Yes, those."

"Well, you know what? How 'bout we cook all these babies up, serve them in a delicious, Italian inspired sauce and see what happens."

After pouring her a glass of ruby red wine, he poured some into the sauce he'd concocted.

Within minutes each shellfish had cracked open, revealing the tender meat inside. Taryn artistically placed a few asparagus spears and glazed carrots onto two plates.

"Dinner is served." Errol spooned the oysters, clams and mussels into two large bowls.

"Certainly smells enticing."

"Have you ever had oysters before?" He took his seat and looked at the uncertain grimace on her face.

"I did… once… a long time ago. It didn't look anything like this."

"Now," Errol said as he picked up a shell and brought it to his mouth. "Let me tell you what I think about this whole aphrodisiac business. While some believe eating oysters will stir your libido, I think…" He slipped his tongue over the quivering mass of flesh atop the shell.

Taryn had the exact reaction he was hoping for. Her eyes widened in shock, narrowed with intrigue then became heavily hooded with a secret longing to see more. He obliged, passing his tongue over the bulbous nub that attached the meat to the shell.

Her lips parted.

Yes, he thought as he watched her with growing interest. Tonight. The cat and mouse game had gone on long enough. He'd played the part of the caring mentor, the dictating chef and the pleasant host.

Now it was time to see what she really had hidden beneath that prim exterior.

He pried apart the black glistening shell of a mussel, exposing the dark meat; the perfect replica of a woman's hidden lips. "Many men like to view this as the taste of a woman. See the resemblance." He slipped his tongue along the tempting folds of flesh.

"So, by your estimation, it's not just oysters, it's all shellfish."

"I guess it's all in the way you look at it." He pried the meat off the shell with a small fork and popped it into his mouth. "I mean, if you really want to examine the issue, let's talk about bananas. Or, let's have a look at that piece of asparagus on your plate."

She poked her fork into the asparagus and brought it to her parted lips.

"Are you inspired?"

Her features crinkled up into a funny grimace. "I get the banana, but this?"

"Try it," he urged, curious to see the workings of her mouth.

She brought the tip of the asparagus into her mouth, closed her lips around it and gently pulled it back out, letting her lips gently stroke it.

It was his turn to stare with hooded eyes. He shifted as his swiftly growing hard-on made him suddenly uncomfortable in his chair. Deeper, he wanted to say, but he let her find her own pace.

Her tongue snaked out to lick dripping butter off the length of the spear then she slowly pushed the vegetable between her pouted lips. It all but disappeared in her mouth before she pulled it out, keeping an enticing amount of pressure of the lucky spear.

"How's that?" she asked with cool innocence.

"Seems you've caught on pretty fast."

She bit the tip of the asparagus off and pointed the remainder at Errol. "I have no idea what you're talking about. I just wanted to lick the delicious butter off before eating it."

He grinned. The blend of naiveté and sensuality she displayed was precisely what he'd been looking for. The women who threw themselves on him were always too easy, too giving, too brash and too obvious. They had no notion of subtlety, no notion of how to play the game. It all made for a boring and predictable chase.

As the dinner progressed, his desire to have her became excruciating. The heat of the evening had brought beads of perspiration to her neck and they now trickled down between her breasts, which he wanted to run his tongue over.

Her face flushed with desire and interest in her plate waned. Her loss of appetite was a clear indicator; something else was on her mind... him.

"A little more wine," he offered as he reached for the bottle.

"I don't think so."

The four little words instantly threw a wrench in his plans. It wasn't the polite refusal of someone who'd already had enough to drink. Her words were heavy and leaden… the begrudged refusal of someone who didn't feel too well.

"You okay?"

"I'm not sure," she admitted.

"Do you want to lie down?"

She passed her hand through the increasingly damp strands of hair that had escaped her ponytail. "That might be a good idea. I'm sorry, Errol," she said as she rose. "I think I might have taken too much wine."

He knew that was impossible. She'd barely touched the second glass he'd poured.

Standing on shaky legs, she kept one hand on the edge of the table and the other over her disturbed belly.

He placed his hand over her forehead. "I think we should get you to the hospital." He stood and took a hold of her arm to steady her.

"Don't be ridiculous. I'm…" Her words faded to nothing just as the blood drained from her face.

"Taryn!"

"I don't feel so good."

He swept her into his arms, grabbed his car keys and hurried out.

*****

"Shellfish can be tricky sometimes," the doctor said as he signed the release form. "Many people fail to prepare them properly and this is the result."

For a second, Errol fumed at the allegations. He was a chef, a world renowned chef. For Pete's sake, he knew how to prepare shellfish. He knew how to prepare virtually anything.

"She's lucky you brought her here so quickly. Had you allowed her to go lie down and try to sleep it off... well, I've seen people get really sick; a lot worse than this."

"I can take her home now?" Errol said as the doctor finished.

"You sure can, but keep her away from anything that could upset her stomach. Nothing too rich, nothing too spicy, nothing too greasy."

Greasy? Didn't this man know who he was? Errol King never served anything greasy.

84

"Keep her diet simple and bland for a few days. She'll appreciate it."

"I will…" Errol said, never ever having gone without adding any seasoning to his meals. He sighed. Taryn Cummings was pushing him in ways he'd never been pushed before. First the waiting for her, and now the change to his way of preparing a meal. He had never been more frustrated, but turned on by a woman.

Chapter 6

"What'd I miss?" Taryn asked the moment Errol walked through the door. She'd been absent from class for two days and couldn't wait to get back. Lying in her bed watching television was something she loathed to do and the thought of missing out on so many classes exacerbated the issue. Though she still felt sluggish and queasy, she hoped to be back on her feet the next day.

"Hygiene," he said with a wry smirk.

"Stop kicking yourself, Errol. These things happen."

"Not to me, they don't." He sat on the edge of her bed and gently put the back of his hand to her forehead.

"I take part of the blame. I kept talking to you, asking a bunch of silly questions. You were distracted."

"I was," he admitted, "but not by your silly questions." His gaze fell into the top of her thin cami as a wicked smile came to his lips.

His smile as well as the smoldering gleam in his eye brought her back to the bath she'd shared with him the day before. Twice she'd drenched the bed sheets with sweat and was in dire need of a good shower, but since standing for any period of time was a risky endeavor, Errol had suggested she take a bath instead.

"Do I have any bedsores yet?" she'd asked as he'd tenderly sponged her back.

He'd laughed and dropped the sponge in the water to then run his bare hand along her skin.

Through the haze of nausea, she'd still felt the stirrings of arousal deep inside. *Why don't you come join me?* The invitation had been a part of her imaginings… or so she thought.

With hooded eyes, she watched him disrobe, fascinated by the lines of his biceps, his chest and the strong muscles of his abs that guided her eyes downward until...

"What are you doing?" she muttered as he stepped into the water. Her eyes remained fixed on the growing hard-on. He was large, larger than she expected, and exquisitely male. What would it feel like to have him in her? What it feel like to wrap her mouth around him? Despite her nervousness and inexperience, she was fascinated.

"I want to make sure you don't drown. Besides, I could use a good bath myself," Errol said sensuously.

"Yeah, I kind of noticed that funk when you helped me out of bed." She offered him a teasing grin.

He chuckled softly, though his eyes seemed more intent on her leg than her comment. His fingers roamed up and down the length of her leg, never straying to her inner thigh. Relieved to see he had a degree of decorum, her body didn't quite agree. It longed to have him touch her where no man had ever been allowed to.

"Do you know how badly I want to make love to you?" He said, his voice deep and hoarse.

A short gasp of shock jammed its way into her throat. She didn't know what to say. He'd been so friendly lately, keeping his distance from her, nothing like the sensuous passion they shared the first day of their arrangement. Aside from a few flirtatious moments, their interactions were innocent, and often businesslike. She was certain he had no interest in her at all. It was as though he had turned off any emotions toward her, and she reacted by focusing harder on her studies. She couldn't fall for him, as big as a crush she had on him from afar, but now with him so close…it was personal.

"I'm sure you say that to all the girls you meet," she finally managed to squeak out. Her breasts tingled with excitement as his roaming fingers continued to work their way up and down her leg, sending jolts of excitement through her.

"I do," he said. His hand dipped down a little further, reaching under her to gently pass his fingers along her buttocks. "But I rarely mean it." His voice was velvety soft, like a gentle caress against her skin.

She let out an involuntary gasp. Despite the subtle waves of nausea that still plagued her, she wanted him. She wanted him to touch her… there, anywhere, softer, harder, more, longer. Anything, so long as his hands never left her.

Like a baker lovingly kneading his dough, Errol reached under her with both hands and caressed her buttocks. Occasionally a stray finger or two would run along the crevice, coming just short of touching the lips that now throbbed with hunger and longing.

Taryn sunk deeper into the tub, offering him easier access to the places she'd always kept to herself. She leaned her head against the back of the bath and closed her eyes, giving her body full reign on the sensations that assaulted it. Had she ever felt anything as blissful? Had her body ever tingled with such life?

No. The joys and thrills she'd experienced so far had been chaste and pure; the joy of a beautiful spring day; the thrill of a spectacular roller coaster ride. Of course there was her first kiss from Jason Campton in fourth grade and the full on make out session with Patrick Stein, but they were innocent adolescent trials. Nothing could compare with the intense thrill of anticipating the next run of Errol's fingers further into un-chartered territory.

But it didn't come. He brought his hands back to her thighs, her knees and her calves, ignoring the fire he'd ignited in her.

"Do you think you'll be strong enough to come back to class tomorrow?" he said.

His tone was annoyingly professional and calm. There was no trace of passion or arousal. To hear him, he'd just finished with the most mundane task.

Frustrated by his lack of true interest, she sat up abruptly. With her eyes on his she let out a bored yawn. "I think I've soaked long enough. I'm starting to pucker."

She reached out to grab her robe. With an air of puritan piety, she looked at him.

Not making any effort to afford her a little privacy, he just sat back to watch her.

"Are you really going to watch?"

"Why not?"

"Decency."

"I think we're past that."

"You might think we are, but I don't."

"Really? And where do you think we are?"

"You're my professor. I'm your student and assistant."

"Hmmm. Funny, I don't remember the last time I shared a bath with a student. However, I do remember one very strange and steamy shower with an assistant some years ago."

She tried to hide her shock, but gaped all the same. In the very next instant, she pressed her lips tightly together and narrowed her eyes in disgust.

"Don't worry. He wasn't my type. Nothing happened."

Shock got the best of her again as she stared wide-eyed at him."

He laughed, loud and hearty. "Oh, for crying out loud, Taryn. I'm kidding."

She stood and, mindless of the puddles of water she left on his clean ceramic floor, got out of the tub, threw the robe over her shoulders and left the bathroom in a huff. God, she had to get out of there or risk throwing herself on him...risk begging him to take her, to plunge himself deep into her so she can satisfy this ache she felt for him.

She wanted him so much…but would she dare admit it to him. She knew once she did, he would consume her, body, mind, and heart.

Chapter 7

Though going to school was still a little too taxing for her, Taryn did manage to catch up on some homework. After a light lunch she pulled out her books and lay them across the dining table. While she was eager to get back to regular classes, there was something cozy about cuddling up in her pajamas in the middle of the day to do her work.

She opened her book to read about the origins of certain recipes and methods of cooking. She'd always presumed there was a certain degree of hit and miss when it came to creating new recipes, but she was surprised to learn of the many lucky accidents that had become French favorites.

Among them was the amusing *Pets de Nonne*. Though the name sounded adorable and elegant in French, the English translation left much to be desired: Nun's Fart. The tasty little ball of dough that was deep fried apparently came about when a nun, shocked and

94

embarrassed by her own bodily gases, dropped the ball of dough in hot oil.

While many contested certain details of the story, Taryn was amused by the notion all the same.

"Busy, busy, busy."

Startled, Taryn threw her pen in the air and almost jumped off her chair. "What are you doing here?" With her hand firmly pressed to her chest to keep her heart from beating its way out, she turned to Errol. "I didn't hear you come in."

"So I see." He looked down at the page she'd been reading. 'I never knew a ball of dough could be so interesting."

"It's fascinating to see where so many of the recipes we take for granted today came from."

"I'm happy to see you're strong enough to study."

"And I'm surprised to see you home so early."

He shrugged. "It's a nice day out. I have a few papers to correct, but I can do that later tonight. I thought I'd take you out for some fresh air."

Taryn sat back and looked at him. She'd been cooped up in his apartment for a number of days, and while the view was breathtaking, going out into the world would do her some good. "I can't promise you I'll be able to go far, but I'd love to get out."

"Come on, then. I have the perfect place to take you."

Trusting him implicitly, she hurried to change into the pretty yellow summer dress she'd not yet had a chance to wear and grabbed her thick green cardigan to fend off the coming chill as the day wore on.

"I must say, it's good to see you out of those pajamas," Errol said as he eyed her with approval.

He guided her down to the streets and turned East on Emeriau then meandered up one street and down another.

"It's such a beautiful city," Taryn mused as she looked all around her. Every street was an endless source of inspiration and awe. She was charmed by the architecture of the homes and awed by the heavenly scents that assailed her nostrils from every bistro. "You must really miss it when you go back to the States."

He nodded as they arrived at the base of the Eiffel Tower. "Few cities can boast of something as spectacular."

Hundreds of people milled around the tower, mostly tourists eager to get a snapshot or take a tour up, but also a lot of locals, stopping for a bite to eat or a relaxed moment in the late afternoon sun.

"How 'bout a ride up?"

"Really?" She looked straight up at the tower. "It's so high. I don't know if I'll be able to stomach the ride."

"I'll be there to catch you if you fall."

"Falling isn't really what I'm concerned about."

"Okay," he said with a wry grin. "I'll be there to pick up after you if you get sick."

As they approached to get a ticket, Taryn sighed with disappointment. "Look, Errol. The sign says they've already sold out for today."

"Stay right here," he ordered.

Before she could protest, he walked away and headed straight to the ticket booth. Moment's later he returned. "Two tickets to the top."

"But... How'd you...?"

"Being a world famous top chef sometimes has its privileges."

They boarded the next elevator with several other tourists.

Feeling a little green, Taryn leaned into Errol as the elevator took off.

"You okay?"

"Yeah." She straightened up and dared a view of the ever shrinking buildings as the elevator rose higher and higher. The horizon was constantly pushed back further offering a view of the *l'Arc de Triomphe* then the parks and homes beyond it until finally all of Paris and beyond came into view.

The ride itself was easy and smooth, but the shaky stop once again had Taryn leaning into Errol. The moment the doors opened, she jumped out, eager to get away from the crowd and breathe an abundance of fresh air. A group of tourists, waiting to return back down, parted like the Red Sea as she plowed through them and rushed to the banister that surrounded the viewing area.

"*Pardonnez-moi*," she said over and over again as she turned to apologize to the crowd.

Most smiled sympathetically, while others openly glared at her. One older woman dared a '*maudite Americaine.*'

"Don't worry about her," Errol said as he came to Taryn's side and put his arm around her.

"Sorry. That last little jump of the elevator nearly did me in."

"I have to admit, I'm happy you were able to contain yourself."

She smiled at him. "Well put."

"Now," he said with mock exasperation. "Enough talk of your tumultuous belly and let's take in this view."

Taryn looked out as far as she could see and let out a dreamy sigh.

"Bet a view from the Empire State Building never looked this good."

"Don't knock the Empire. It's pretty iconic in its own right."

"I'm just saying…"

"It is beautiful," she admitted as she turned to face the cool breeze.

"Come on. Let's see what the other side has to offer."

A young amorous couple leaned against the banister, their eyes melting over one another. Standing almost nose to nose, it was clear no one around them existed. They were alone in their own romantic little world.

"Let's leave them alone," Taryn suggested as she turned to go the other way.

"Newlyweds," Errol said with an indignant huff. "The place is full of them. Or maybe they just got engaged. If the sucker only knew what he was getting himself into."

Taryn shot him a nasty glare. "How romantic of you," she spat.

They came upon a view of Pont Alexandre III and Montmartre in the distance, and Taryn was swept away by the romanticism of it all. How perfectly spectacular, she thought.

"I'm a pragmatic realist," he argued as he gazed at the famed Chateau.

"You don't believe in marriage?" She'd heard he was an elusive bachelor but had never really thought he was so dead set against marriage.

"Believe? What's to believe? You get hitched because some woman wants a damned ring on her finger and all the fluff that goes with a wedding." He looked pointedly at her. "You wannabe princesses all want that damned wedding. What's the deal? If half the women out there put as much effort into actually pleasing the guy they claim to love enough to put through this farce as they do into the farce of the wedding itself, maybe the divorce rate wouldn't be what it is."

"Wow," she droned. "What a sad take on something so beautiful."

He leaned over the banister and looked straight down. "If it's really that beautiful, why do more than half of them end with fighting and hating?"

She didn't know what to say. Her view of marriage had always been a little magical, like most girls. She had her own dreams of walking into Kleinfeld's and picking out the perfect Pnina Tornai dress. She'd envisioned the flowers, the venue, the food. The reception hall would be in white and silver, and she'd often flirted with the notion of a color theme for all the guests. Her bridesmaid would…

Oh my God. Errol was right, she thought with dismal frankness.

"You're just now waking up to the realization, aren't you?"

She blushed as she saw him looking intently at her.

"I saw it," he said as he drew his finger in the air around her face. "That look in your eyes. You've had those fairytale dreams, too, haven't you?"

Shrugging off his accusation, she turned to Paris. "When I was six, maybe, but since then I've grown up and I have a more adult view of marriage. Of course, I know there are a lot of divorces out there, but that still doesn't mean a happy marriage can't exist."

"For six months, top. After that you just have a couple who tries to pretend they want to be together. Before long they're barely able to stand being in the same room together. Then it's just a matter of having an affair right then and there, thereby stretching the marriage out a little longer, or doing the honorable thing and calling it quits before anyone really gets hurt."

Dumbfounded, she looked at him.

"Don't look at me like that, honey. I'm not unhappy knowing all this."

"But, what do you have to look forward to if not meeting someone you can love and trust and spend the rest of your life with?"

Taking a hold of her elbow, he led her along the walkway and let out a little laugh. "Give yourself a few years and a few relationships, and you'll see exactly what I mean."

A denser crowd occupied the west side of the tower and Taryn wondered what the fuss was all about, until she caught sight of the golden rays of the fading sun that lit the sky.

"Sunset over Paris," Errol said. "There's nothing like it."

Taryn tried to get a better view, but there were too many heads in front of her.

"Here." Errol pulled her back to the elevator. "I have an idea."

"But the sunset…"

"I know where we can have a perfect, undisturbed view of the sunset, all while enjoying a perfect glass of Pinot Noire." He turned to the elevator operator. *"Le Jules Verne."*

"We won't have time, Errol." She grabbed the side of the elevator as it jolted into motion. "In another twenty minutes the sun will be completely over the horizon."

"In two minutes we'll be sitting at one of the finest restaurants in all of Paris, and we'll enjoy the best view Paris has to offer."

The doors opened and Errol guided her to one of the most famed restaurants in all of Europe. She'd not paid attention when he'd mentioned Jules Verne, but now she remembered. It was the restaurant all tourists dreamed of eating at, while few could either afford the French menu or acquire a reservation.

In hushed tones Errol spoke to the maitre'd who smiled, checked his list then guided them to a quiet table with a breathtaking view.

"How's that for a sunset?" Errol said as he pulled back her chair.

Feeling like the princess he'd scorned just moments earlier, she sat down. "I never would have believe I'd be sitting here at Jules Verne. It's unreal."

"Wait until you try their *langoustines*

While Taryn took in the view, Errol ordered a bottle of wine.

"I take it you approve," he said.

She turned to face him. "Isn't it a little ironic that you, the self-professed hater of all that is love, marriage and romance, should take me out to dinner in one, if not, the most romantic restaurant in the world. Do you have any idea how many people get engaged here?"

With a cockeyed grin, he picked up the menu and scrutinized it. "Just because people want to foolishly turn this gastronomical heaven into some Parisian tunnel of love…"

"You know, you're really too cynical for someone your age."

*****

After dinner they took a private staircase to the second level and strolled at their leisure. The sky had just turned its last shade of deep purple before succumbing to the darkness of night and the City of Lights sparked to life.

"Oh, my God. Errol…" She gently reached out to touch his hand. "Look how beautiful…" She wanted to weep at the beauty of this day, the perfect afternoon, the wondrous dinner and the spectacular night show.

She expected him to groan his disdain of romance again, but instead, he leaned into her and tenderly kissed her brow. They remained silent as they took in all the night had to offer.

When a cooled chill blew by them Errol gave her hand a tug. "How 'bout a touch of sweetness to finish this off."

The dessert was the perfect finish to their gastronomical meal. From beginning to end, dinner was everything the Jules Verne reputation promised; the food, elegantly plated and delicious; the view exquisite and unforgettable; the service impeccable.

"What I wouldn't give to work in such a restaurant," Taryn said as they later walked along the darkened streets below *la Tour Eiffel*.

Paris came alive at night. The lights, music and aromas all there to tempt the senses.

"I would have thought your aspirations ran higher," Errol said. "Like owning a restaurant such as Le Jules Verne."

She chuckled and leaned playfully into him. "You're right. I do dream of owning such a restaurant… of turning the restaurant back home into the kind of place people dream of dining at."

For a brief moment he put his arm around her and pulled her in tight before releasing her. "Do I hear a hint of doubt in that dream?"

Surprised, she looked up at him. "Do you?"

He shrugged. "There was a definite lack of conviction."

"Hmmm." She considered her words. Did she really have any doubt she'd succeed in building the reputation of her little family-owned restaurant into something like *Le Jules Verne*? "I know I have talent," she finally said. "I know my way around the kitchen.

I know how to bring out the flavors in food without overdoing it. I know many of the techniques that make for great haute cuisine. I certainly have the passion to go on learning what I don't already know."

"But...?"

She stopped and turned to face him. "After eating something as divinely perfect as what I ate tonight... I don't know. I guess I just really wonder if I have what it takes to make it that far."

Taking her hand in his he led her onto the paved path that ran along the Seine. "A little doubt can be good... keeps you on your toes... keeps you hungry and eager to learn... keeps you fighting for perfection. There's nothing worse than complacency; than sitting on your laurels. Some of the best chefs lose their way because they allow themselves to think they know everything. We never know everything. Cooking is a constantly changing art. Just don't let that little taste of doubt get the best of you. It can demolish you faster than you can collapse a soufflé."

Hand in hand they walked along the river. Quaint streetlamps offered a minimal glow on the water, just enough to make for a romantic stroll. Taryn basked in the pleasant silence that enveloped them. Occasionally they crossed paths with other couples; couples who were obviously in love.

Taryn involuntarily squeezed Errol's hand and wondered.

*****

While the dinner had been all and more than Errol had expected of his greatest competition, a regrettable little voice at the back of his head persisted in reminding him that it was because of her.

Taryn delighted him, more than he cared to admit.

As they strolled along the Seine, he knew they were surrounded by the romance Paris promised. Repeatedly, he told himself to let go of her hand, to shove his hands deep into his pockets and simply walked along the famed river as two friends, as two associates.

But her hand was soft and warm... and that little squeeze. What had caused her to spontaneously squeeze his hand like that?

109

You're getting in too deep, his heart warned.

No, the depth of his loin reminded him. Women love to be romanced, to be wooed. He'd seen it in her eyes; despite his anti-marriage monologue, she still had dreams of a white dress and fairytale ending.

How mistaken she was if she thought her time with him would end happily ever after. No, tonight... this evening... it was the perfect prerequisite for a heated night of sexually tantalizing games... nothing more.

Chapter 8

"The idea behind this is I want the outside to be crispy without being crunchy while inside we find a warm… goo," Errol said.

Leaning into the kitchen counter, Taryn let out an amused chuckle. "Goo? Is that the official term for it?"

Errol looked sidelong at her, his face a mask of professionalism. "As a matter of fact, I had considered giving the term some validity."

"Errol King's goo… sounds like it'll take off. Before long everyone will be making Errol King's goo with its crispy but not crunchy exterior."

"You mock me, my dear assistant."

Though he remained stiff and unsmiling, she knew he was toying with her. She'd come to know the little known comic side he hid from the world. Heaven forbid the world should discover that Chef King had a bonafide sense of humor.

"Not at all," she said with a haughty air. "I think goo suits the purpose perfectly."

They'd tried several variations of the recipe Errol wanted to add to his cookbook, but could still not get the consistency he sought. More salt. Less baking powder. More sodium bicarbonate. Less sugar. Hotter oven. Shorter time. Cool before putting into oven. Cool immediately out of the oven.

Finally, Taryn said, "What if we were to brush a little sweetened melted butter over it before popping it into the oven?"

Errol grimaced.

"What?" she said incredulously. "I think that's a perfectly good suggestion."

"Sweetened with what?"

She thought for a moment. She knew he would balk at plain white sugar, and brown sugar wouldn't be much better. No, it would have to be a liquid sweetener. "How 'bout honey?"

"Too common."

"Molasses?"

He grimaced. "Too vulgar."

"Maple syrup?"

"Too hard to come by."

"Isn't that the whole idea?" She opened the pantry door and peered inside. Among the various bottles of fancy oils and vinegars, the many jars of rare ingredients, spices and herbs and the few more common every day items, she found a bottle of molasses. "I just found something rather vulgar in your pantry, Errol."

He cocked a brow as he looked at her. A boyish grin made a quick appearance on his face before dashing off to leave room for a smirk. "Just because I enjoy a little molasses on my buckwheat pancakes every once in a while doesn't mean it's a good idea for this recipe."

"Buckwheat pancakes? You?"

"Just because I'm a culinary genius doesn't mean I can't enjoy a little comfort food once in a while."

Taryn grabbed the bottle of molasses and brought it to their working space. "I think this will work. Are you ready to give it a shot?"

He looked at the bottle then at her. "I honestly don't think the flavor is going to harmonize well with the..."

"Goo?" she finished for him.

"Right," he said with a chuckle.

Ignoring his doubt and skepticism, Taryn placed a small saucepan on the stovetop, threw in a generous pat of butter and gently melted it. When it was reduced to a golden liquid, she opened the bottle of molasses. "Just a soupcon," she said as she poured a small dollop in.

"Why do I have a feeling you're about to ruin the last batch?"

"Because you're a cynical old man hiding in the body of..." She caught herself and looked sheepishly at him.

"The body of...?" he said as he rolled his hand in the air, urging her to continue.

With a nonchalant shrug she dipped her pastry brush into the now black butter. "The body of a young guy. That's all."

"Hmm." He watched the workings of her brush. "I'm not really sure that's the look I was going for."

"Once it's cooked, it won't look that bad."

"We'll see."

With a very Parisian 'voila,' Taryn opened the oven, popped in the cookie sheet and shut the door. "In eight minutes you'll have your crispy goo."

Facing one another, they leaned against the counter, waiting.

"You know, if this doesn't work out, I have half a mind to shower you with the remainder of that molasses."

"In…" In dramatic fashion, Taryn raised her wrist to her face and looked at her watch. "Four minutes, *mon cher Errol*, I'll make you eat your words."

"Of course you will. I'll have nothing else to eat because you'll have ruined my last batch." Grinning, he drummed his fingers on the stovetop.

"Why, the nerve…" She pushed the rolling pin aside and picked up a fistful of flour.

"Ah, ah, ah," Errol chanted as he waved a finger at her. "I wouldn't do that if I were you."

"No," she argued. "If it were you, you would have pushed the flour aside and tossed me the rolling pin."

He bellowed with laughter, a laugh that came from the depths of his being; a laugh that was innocent and playful; a laugh she'd never heard before.

"I think you're getting to know me a little too well." He looked at his watch. "The moment of truth has arrived."

Taryn threw her fistful of flour on the counter and clapped her hands clean. Feeling triumphant, she opened the oven door, but quickly shut it again.

"What's the matter?" Errol said with a knowing grin.

"They're not ready yet."

"That's impossible. They've been in there the full eight minutes." He reached for the oven door.

"I said they're not ready." Putting her hand over his she tried to keep him from opening the door.

"Another few minutes won't salvage your disaster, Taryn." He opened the door and smiled as he pulled out the cookie sheet. "Perhaps when I mentioned that I wanted them crispy and not crunchy, I should have also mentioned that I wanted them golden… not tarred."

She looked at the unappetizing result of her inspiration. "Sorry."

His eyes hardened with displeasure. "I think you can take your apron off now," he said in a tone that nearly demolished her. "You're finished here."

"Errol…" She hesitated a moment, remembering she'd not put on a bra under her cami that morning. Another harsh glare from Errol, however, and she untied her apron, pulled it over her head and set it on the counter. "I was only trying to…"

He put up a silencing finger.

"Do you want me to leave?"

"On the contrary. I want you to stay and learn."

He set the cookie sheet on the stove and reached for the bottle of molasses. Turning the bottle over, he read the label then tilted the bottle one side and the other, letting the thick liquid run along the walls of the bottle.

Watching him, she tried to gauge his mood. Was he truly disappointed in the result? Angry even? Or was he toying with her?

With a quick sniff in the air, he looked into the saucepan she'd used then dipped his finger into the buttery molasses. He looked at it, smelled it then tasted it. Without saying a word, he wiped his finger off on a towel then uncapped the bottle and smelled it.

As if looking for something, he ran his finger along the edge of the bottle cleaning off the few sticky drops that remained. He licked his finger, flapping his lips together as he tasted. "I guess there is a certain…" He puckered and swished his tongue around his mouth. "A certain *je ne sais quoi* about the flavor of molasses."

"Just because they look a little funny doesn't mean they won't taste good," Taryn said with complete lack of conviction. "Why don't you try…?"

Errol put his hand up to quiet her and continued to examine the bottle of molasses. "Dark, sticky, sweet," he murmured. He turned the bottle upside down and let a large dollop drop over his fingers.

Glaring at her, he held up his molasses covered fingers. "Do you see how utterly opaque this is?"

"Yes," she muttered.

"You can't even see my fingers through this black goo."

"I thought that, maybe, with the melted butter it would…"

"Honey is golden and translucent. Maple syrup is amber and clear. But this…?"

"I'll be sure never to make the same mistake again."

Without warning, Errol reached out and slathered the molasses over her chest from one shoulder to the other.

"I want you to remember this day, Taryn."

"I will." She glanced down. The molasses had already reached the top of her white cami. She didn't know whether she should feel humiliated or infuriated.

He brought the bottle above her heaving breasts and let the thick dark liquid slide into her cami. "I want you to remember how molasses looks… how it feels."

Saying nothing, she felt the sticky liquid make its slow descent between her breasts.

"How does it feel, Taryn?" His voice had dropped to a deep, smoldering tone.

"Wet," she whispered.

He brought the bottle up to her shoulder and poured the remaining content.

"Wet and…?"

"Sticky."

Licking his lips, he set the bottle down on the counter and scrutinized her. "Wet, sticky, and…?"

She looked at him, looked into his eyes and tried to see… What did he want from her?

"Wet, sticky, and…?" he repeated.

"Sweet?" she ventured.

He brought his hand to her shoulder and rubbed the molasses over her skin. With dainty fingers, he pulled up the thin straps of her cami and let them fall over her shoulders. His hands continued to work the black syrup around and around. "You hardly look sweet, my dear."

His voice had turned husky, almost dark and Taryn knew the game had changed. It was no longer a matter of an angry professor berating a clumsy student, or the irate chef degrading his assistant.

The temperature in the room suddenly rose, as did Taryn's chest as it heaved with labored breaths.

120

Her breasts were on alert, her nipples nudging relentlessly at the thin fabric of her cami.

"No, my dear…" Errol took a hold of the straps of her cami once more and pulled them down past her elbows, exposing her breasts as he did so. He let out a brief gasp of excitement, but quickly contained himself. With hooded eyes and parted lips, he brought his sticky, black hands over her breasts, covering them until they were glossy. "You are dirty. You are exquisitely dirty."

Taryn swallowed the ball of confusion that nearly left her drooling. Her body cried out with so many conflicting messages, she didn't know how to react. This wasn't supposed to happen. He wasn't supposed to touch her like this, and she should stop him.

But his hands… She inhaled, pressing her breasts further into his hands, hands that were warm, hands that were gentle, hands that made her feel…

"Do you feel dirty, Taryn?"

Her lips parted and her tongue toyed with the notion of coming out, but not to speak. There were no words. Her tongue wanted him, wanted to taste him.

His thumbs flickered over her erect nipples, and Taryn let out a wanton groan as a pulsating wave of ecstasy gathered between her thighs.

"Yes," he sighed. "You do feel dirty, don't you?"

He brought his hands to the small of her back, bringing her closer. The slight pressure of his hands arched her back, making it easier for him to sweep his mouth over her breast. The tip of his tongue circled around, slow and teasing as it licked off some of the molasses.

Groaning from deep in his throat, he leaned back to look at his handiwork. He licked his lips and tilted his head to the side as he looked at her.

Taryn looked down at her milky white breast, now clearly visible under the thinned veil of black sugar. She swallowed the lump of uncertainty as she met Errol's gaze. Something playful lingered in his gaze, teasing… almost mocking.

"I think I should…" Taryn choked out as she considered putting an end to this game.

Before she could finish her thought, Errol leaned in and licked the underside of her breast, this time using the full breadth of his tongue. He swept his tongue over her nipple and onward to her collar bone. But it was her nipple who begged for more attention.

"Errol," she groaned. Her head fell back as her fingers raked through his hair and led him back to her nipple.

He obliged, and suckled; hard and pulling one moment; gentle and teasing the next. Taryn reached back to lean against the counter as he traveled through the valley of her breasts to assault the other nipple. Her legs were about to give out on her as an explosion of sensations threatened to bubble over.

Breathless, Errol pulled back, his face smeared in black. The playfulness was gone and his eyes reflected the urgency they both felt. He looked down at her breasts and brought his hands around her waist to smudge molasses along her belly.

"Beautiful," he muttered. He reached for the fastenings of her jeans and quickly peeled them off. "Beautiful."

Her cotton underwear were damp with want and she felt a blush of embarrassment rise to her cheeks. Would he think her odd or strange because she had such a lack of control over her body?

With a soiled finger, he pulled back the top elastic band of her panties and looked inside. "The more I discover of you the more beautiful you get." He shoved both hands in and reached around to grab her ass. "I think we've gotten ourselves into a real sticky mess," he whispered as he leaned into her, burying his face into her folds and licking her with long savoring strokes.

Taryn arched her back and push her pelvis closer to him, clenching her teeth to keep from screaming with pleasure. Errol's tongue devouring her, his teeth grazing against her sensitive nub was sending her to a point she'd never experienced before…to a point she no longer had any control of her body. She convulsed, shuddered, and shook with an intense pressure of pleasure, it rocked her to the core. "Oh God, Errol," she cried.

"So responsive," Errol grinned, looking up at her where he was now lightly stroking her with his long fingers. "And so beautifully dirty."

"Like I was trying to say earlier," she finally managed to utter between breaths and shudders. "I think I should take a shower."

"Good idea," Errol said, tearing off the remainder of her clothes.

He looked down his molasses-soiled shirt and strip down to nothing except his hardness, and said, "There is no way I'm not joining you in the showers now."

Chapter 9

Before the alarm clock went off, Taryn was awakened by a subtle but insistent movement in the bed. It was Errol who nudged his hard erection against her backside. Smiling, she cracked her eyes open, eager to have him take her again.

"I should be sated," he whispered into her ear. "I should be exhausted, but I don't think I can stop wanting more of you."

The night had indeed been exhausting.

After a long and titillating shower, Errol had sat her on the bathroom counter and gently parted her legs. With bated breath, she'd watched him, intrigued... eager. He'd already brought her such wondrous sensations with his mouth and fingers while he washed her in the shower. What more did he have in store?

But she could never have imagined the sensations to come. Errol brought his mouth, warm and wet, to a heavenly little nub of flesh she'd never

126

known existed until that night. Stunned by the initial sensation, so intense, so pleasurable, Taryn let out a small cry of surprise, grabbed the edge of the counter and leaned back.

"Oh, my God," she let out as he continued to run his tongue along the flesh that was now so exquisitely alive. "Oh, Errol."

"Oh!" Her cry, foreign and feral, echoed in the bathroom as her body was elevated to a level of pleasure that seemed impossible. She hovered there for a moment, an exquisite moment of breathlessness, of waiting for the ultimate.

Errol gripped her hips, tight and fierce as his tongue made the final assault. With one long, slow, delicious lick, Taryn's body exploded in a rapture of ecstasy. She dug her fingers into his hair, keeping his mouth pressed to hers as her body moved, convulsed with a will of its own. Her legs straightened out, down to the tips of her toes.

Before her body could stop throbbing, Errol straightened up and plunged his erection deep inside her, filling her. Her eyes widened as a short, sharp pain cut into her pleasure, then subsided, replaced by the feeling of fullness and intense sensation of him rocking in and out of her until he came, groaning with his release.

Now, as she lay beside him, the heat of his body warming hers, she longed to relive every stroke, every lick, and every tantalizingly fucking again.

Errol slid his hand between her thighs and quickly aroused her. "I don't want to push you to do too much too fast."

After that first, quick romp in the bathroom, they'd made love again, slower and longer. They'd finally fallen asleep in each others' arms, only to awaken a few hours later when they began anew. Insatiable for each other, and wanting this from the first day they met.

"Then let me push you." She turned to face him then rose to straddle him.

He cocked a brow of interest as he watched her. "My innocent virgin, do you know what to do up there?"

"I'll figure it out," she said with a teasing lick of her lips.

With an intense gaze fixed on her inner thighs, Errol propped himself up on a pillow, clasped his fingers together and brought them behind his head.

Suddenly self-conscious, Taryn wondered if she'd not taken on more than she could handle. Uncertain of her moves, she nestled over his hardness. Though she longed to have him inside her, simply gliding over the length of him brought her a degree of pleasure.

She looked at Errol to gauge his appreciation. His eyes narrowed and his tongue played on the edge of his lips, but he remained somewhat aloof.

For a moment she considered abandoning all efforts, but her body wasn't quite ready to let go just yet. If there was one thing she'd learned over the course of the night, it was the intense pleasure of an orgasm and how to attain it. With slow, methodical movements, she sought her own pleasure, using her fingers to tease her nipples, while she glided over him repeatedly, sliding back and forth over the length of his erection, causing him to groan. The rising crescendo of her orgasm came quickly, surprisingly quick. Closing her eyes, she leaned back and let the waves of her orgasm sweep over her.

"You're being selfish," Errol accused in a throaty voice that dripped with arousal. He reached up to grab her breasts, his fingers hungry, almost angry. "Don't toy with me. I've waited too long to thoroughly fuck you. I'm still not through with you yet."

Still riding the ebbing ripples of her ecstasy, she looked at him and murmured, "I don't want to push you to do too much, too fast."

"Never." With a force and speed that surprised her, he gripped her by the waist, threw her back on the bed and mounted her, driving deep until she let out a guttural moan. With savage thrusts he pounded out his need, gripping her breasts, while rotating his hips with each stroke, groaning loudly like a beast. Her head was spinning with the unbelievable ecstasy of him filling her to the brink, only to empty out and plunge back in, each stroke bringing her almost to the brink of climax. With one final earth-shattering thrust, he quickly erupted inside her, filling her, while she climaxed, shuddering all around her. He kissed her savagely on her lips, gripping her breasts as he plucked her nipples, and said, "Mine."

After a surprisingly brief amount of time, he rose. "Time to get to school." Without looking back at her, he headed to the shower.

Taryn remained in bed, letting the sensations fade away, but as they did, reality set it. For a long moment she sat mulling over the more serious implications of their night together. She'd abandoned all concern for the consequences and had allowed the pleasures of her body to take priority. Now she faced them head on.

"Aren't you going to get ready?" Errol said as he emerged from the bathroom, damp and glistening in all his glory.

"Oh God, Errol. We didn't...we didn't use precaution. What if I get pregnant?" she asked.

"You won't," he called out.

"You've had so many lovers, what if I catch something from you?"

He walked out, dressed in charcoal slacks and a white shirt. Occupied with the knotting of his tie, he didn't look up at her. "I won't give you anything."

"How do you know?"

Making the final adjustments on his tie, he looked at her, his eyes hooded with boredom. "Because I know. I'm clean. I live cleanly, and I'm tested, but I'm not going into that now. Now get up and get dressed. You're late."

Unsatisfied with his answer, she got out of bed and took a quick shower. By the time she came out, he was gone.

Chapter 10

"If you look at this plate, what do you see?" Errol stood at the front of the class, a cellophane covered dish on the desk in front of him.

Seething as she'd gotten out of her taxi, she'd hoped to have a chance to berate him for leaving her in such a way. She might be innocent when it came to such games, but she wasn't about to let him treat her like some... some slut. It'd taken every French swear word she could think of to get the driver to hurry up, all so she could run into the school breathless and slip into class in the nick of time.

His gaze briefly darted to her when she entered, but he was otherwise the professional she'd come to know in class.

"Pureed potatoes," one student called out.

"Shredded chicken in a creamy sauce," other one said.

"Those look like overcooked carrots."

"And all together, what do you have?" Errol asked.

"Dinner at my grandmother's house," one bold student dared.

Errol grinned. "Right. A plate of mush... bland mush at that." Clasping his hands together he came around his desk and leaned back, crossing his long legs out in front of him.

Taryn tried not to imagine the heated moments they'd shared that morning and tried to concentrate on what he said.

"Today we're going to look at textures, colors and even shapes as we bring a plate together."

Finally able to bring her thoughts to the task at hand, Taryn took notes and managed to be attentive throughout the class. Only when Errol, strolling among the students, came to pass behind her and gently brush his hand along her rear end did she falter.

She was excited to see she still interested him, but could have slapped him for risking such a move right there in class.

"Chef King." The dual supremacy of his name echoed in the air as Taryn called out to him at the end of the lesson.   As the class emptied, she made her way to his desk. "I hope you'll understand how important this all is to me."

He sat behind his desk, clasped his hand over his belly and looked up at her. "I would like to think my classes are important to everyone here."

"I just want to make it clear." She set both hands on his desk and leaned forward, hoping to get through to him.   "My scholarship here means everything to me."

"I'll keep that in mind."

"I would hate to put it in jeopardy because you insist on playing your silly games."

He rose to face her as a wicked grin took hold of his lips. "They didn't seem that silly this morning."

A streak of blush heated her cheeks. At first the responsibility fell on the flash memory of that morning, but she quickly realized it was also the infuriating manner in which he made light of the situation she now found herself in.

His hand crept along the top of the desk until the tips of his fingers met hers. She recoiled with surprising speed. For a moment she considered her

135

options. She could threaten to move out of his apartment; that was hardly viable. She could threaten to report him. Who would believe *he* was harassing *her*? In anything, they'd accuse her of stalking him.

Crossing her arms in front of her, she looked at him. "Please, Errol," she said softly.

A wistful smile came to his lips and his eyes softened. "I wouldn't dream of doing anything that could ruin your chances of attaining your goals."

"I'm glad we understand each other. Thank you." Before he could say more, she turned and left the room.

That night, as she waited for him to arrive, she contemplated the situation she'd gotten herself into. Errol King was a handsome, charismatic, if not enigmatic man who thrilled her in ways she never would have imagined.

Yet, she felt she'd allowed herself to play in a game she couldn't win.

Since arriving after school, she'd changed clothes three times; out of her school clothes and into lace panties and a semi-transparent blouse. Too obvious, she argued. He'll think he'd won. Going to the opposite spectrum, she'd pulled on unflattering sweatpants and an oversized t-shirt. Again, too obvious, she thought. He'd think she was deliberately trying to downplay their affair.

In the end, she opted for her dressy pajamas. Blue and white striped cotton, they were legitimately relaxed enough for a cozy night at home without any hint of sexuality. The message would be clear; their sexual liaison was over.

She settled in on the sofa, plugged the television to a food channel and opened her French technique book on her lap. The moment she heard the doorknob rattle, however, she looked down at her dowdy pajamas and wondered if this was really the message she wanted to send him. Did she really want it to be over? As the door opened, her skin tingled. As his footsteps approached, her body heated up.

"Nice try," he said.

The sound of his voice, deep, masculine and sensual flowed over her like a velvet hand, soothing her and making her forget the promise she'd made to herself; it was over.

She turned to him, her face a mask that hid the sexual tension she felt inside; at least that's what she hoped he'd see.

"Those pajamas," he went on. "If you're trying to dissuade me from seducing you tonight, you've failed miserably."

Getting to her feet, she was pleased and disappointed. "And if you think you'll succeed in sedu..."

He took one forceful step toward her, wrapped his hand around the nape of her neck and pulled her in to kiss her. Her resolve melted in that instant, and when his tongue swept over hers and she tasted his hunger, all she wanted was his body pressed against hers.

Through the heated kiss, he yanked off the bottom of her pajamas, tore off her panties and grabbed her legs to pull her up and wrap her legs around his waist. With a tight hold around his neck, she held on as he carried her to the dining table.

His kisses plundered her neck, and down to the valley of her breasts. With a savage roar, he grabbed each panel of her top and pulled it apart, sending

138

buttons flying across the room. Her breasts, exposed and heaving with the need to be touched, begged for his attention.

"Tell me you haven't been thinking of this very moment all day," he challenged. His mouth clamped onto a breast and drew an orgasmic cry out of Taryn. "Tell me the day wasn't endless and tortured with wanting me."

He hurriedly pulled off his shirt and unfastened his pants to let them pool at his feet.

In a brief moment of lucidity, Taryn put her hand to his chest to stop him. "Tell me what you would do if I were to stop you... right now."

Amusement played in his eyes, though they smoldered with undeniable passion. "Would you, Taryn?" He smiled, that wicked smile that weakened her every time.

"Errol...I can't," she whispered. "I want you in me too much, even if I try."

He leaned in close. "Then just try to stop me," he whispered hoarsely as he buried his erection in the soft, moist folds of flesh that awaited him. "Try to stop me," he repeated as he continued his plunge, deeper and fuller each time, taking her breath away with each thrust.

All sense of pride and propriety left her as she screamed out her pleasure and clung to him for more. Only when he stopped, sweaty, his hair rumpled in front of his face, and spent, did she look soberly at him. She leaned back, her elbows propped up on the table and felt strangely free and vulnerable at the same time.

"I'll readily admit I enjoy this game, Errol. You do things to me I never could have imagined. And, yes, okay, I did spend the better part of the day thinking about this moment, but I need you to be more specific with your answer."

"Answer to what?" Still hooded with the remains of lust, his eyes barely focused on her.

"You're not doing anything to protect me. You're not taking any precautions."

"What precaution? Protect you from what?"

She gazed down at their joined pelvises, the sight causing her to become aroused again. "Pregnancy. Sexually transmit…"

"That again? I told you not to worry about that."

"Easy for you to say. You're not the one at risk."

"Look, there's no way you can get pregnant because… well, I already took care of that, besides it's both of us at risk…I would not leave a woman not taken care of."

Stunned, she looked at him. "But you're so young."

He rolled his eyes to the ceiling. "As for the other stuff; one, I'm careful; two, I'm tested and three, I'm not as slutty as the media sometimes makes me out to be." He looked hurt for a while, "I do care about the women I'm with, Taryn. I may like it rough, but I always take care of my lovers."

She took a moment to take in his words. "Okay," she finally said. "What about my scholarship?"

"I told you earlier." He cupped her cheek and brought a sober gaze to meet her eyes. "I wouldn't do anything to jeopardize that. Besides, you wanted this arrangement, as much as I did. You said so yourself when I asked in the beginning."

Taryn looked down. It was true…she wanted this just as much as he did.

Errol brought a finger to her chin to lift it up so her eyes were looking into his blue ones. "You do want this, don't you?" His thumb played with the full flesh of her lower lips, making her want to take in his thumb and taste him. God, his mere touch was enough to make her want to climb all over him and ride him until they were both sweaty and exhausted from passionate lovemaking.

Errol's voice was husky but soft against her ear. "You do want me, Taryn, don't you? I can see the desire in your eyes…you want me now." He replaced his thumb with his lips on her lip, and nibbled on her lower lip, sucking it until they were swollen. Then he moved his mouth over hers, plunging his tongue in to taste her tongue, while his fingers found her folds below, dipping in and out until she was writhing against him.

"Yes," she cried. "Yes, God, yes! I want you, Errol. Now!"

He positioned himself against her, rubbing her clit with his shaft before plunging deep inside of her. He rocked against her back and forth, gyrating his hips, causing her to moan with intense pleasure. Soon they were making love in every part of the apartment, their passion for each other insatiable.

Errol was true to his word as the weeks passed. Taryn felt safe with him, in every way, and even became the instigator of their sexual games in many instances. In class, she deliberately toyed with him, running her fingers along a stiff rod of dough in a suggestive way, and licking cream off her fingers while she eyed him from across the room.

On more than one occasion she caught him heading to his desk to readjust his arousal. Today, he discreetly brushed that arousal along her back side as he helped her.

"You're being too rough with the cream," he said as he stood behind her and rearranged her hand on the whisk. "You have to…"

She didn't hear a word of what he said. All she knew was the clear and unmistakable pressure of his hard-on against her back, that instantly made her wet.

That night they didn't speak a word to one another, but quickly engaged in the animal dance that occupied so many of their nights. There were no formalities or niceties, just an endless hunger that kept them clamped to one another until they were too exhausted to go on anymore.

Every night following was filled with wild passionate lovemaking. She couldn't get enough of him, and her body craved him like food.

"I can devour you all day," Errol said, one lazy Sunday as they stayed in bed, making love from morning to night.

"Then devour me," Taryn said, huskily.

Errol grinned wickedly. "You don't have to ask. Your taste is a constant aphrodisiac for me, Taryn."

Still glowing from the effects of their white hot sex, the next morning, Taryn rolled off the bed to get the phone that ringed with persistence. It'd rung twice during their love making, but they'd disregarded it.

"It's for you, *Monsieur King*," she said as she held the phone out to him. Standing nude before him, she already anticipated his next hard-on.

144

With a knowing grin, he ran his finger along the thin line of hair between her thighs then took the phone. *"Oui. Oui c'est bien ca."* He fell silent and furrowed his brow as he listened. His eyes reddened as tears gathered. *"Comment? Mais, elle est... Oui."*

Hearing the emotion in his voice, Taryn sat beside him and waited. The husky, sexually charged man he'd been just seconds ago now sat lost in the middle of the bed, like a little boy.

"Oui, je comprend." Keeping his eyes on the bed sheets in front of him, he absentmindedly played with the corner of his pillow. *"Tres bien. J'arrive."*

"What's the matter?" Taryn asked, taking his hand. She had never seen him so down and sad as he was at that moment. "Please tell me, Errol."

Errol stared straight ahead of him, his entire face broken.

"My nana," he said. "She passed away last night."

Chapter 11

Though she always made sure she remained just one step behind him, Taryn accompanied Errol to his grandmother's funeral. While he appeared strong and stoic to all those in attendance, Taryn knew just how fragile his mental state was. Since receiving the phone call he'd barely spoken a word to her. He'd barely spoken at all.

He'd found himself with the regrettable task of arranging his Nana's service; nothing less than the Notre Dame Cathedral for his beloved grandmother. "If there's anything I can do," Taryn had offered.

Pressing his lips together, he'd shaken his head. "It's my responsibility. Besides, it's all in French. There's little you can do."

Feeling shut out, Taryn busied herself around the apartment. She prepared meals that went uneaten by Errol and picked up after him. In the brief week between learning of his Nana's death and the finality of the service, he'd visibly lost weight. The day of the service, he was gaunt and pale.

"*Notre Pere qui es aux cieux,*" the priest said from the pulpit.

Dressed in somber black, Taryn sat in the row behind Errol. "Our Father who art in heaven…" She murmured the Father's Prayer in English as everyone around her prayed in French. "… Give us this day our daily bread…"

"… *mais deliver-nous du mal.*"

"Amen," everyone murmured in unison. Many associates from the Institute had come, as well as a few elderly and distant family members, friends of his grandmother's and some acquaintances.

At the end of the service, Taryn put her hand to Errol's shoulder. He looked back at her, an appreciative, but tight smile on his face.

For an interminable hour he stood at the doors of the cathedral, receiving words of condolences, praise of his Nana's life and encouragement to move on. He nodded, smiled and even offered a few words of solace and comfort to a few friends overwrought with emotion.

"Want me to drive you home?" Taryn asked Errol when the last mourner walked away.

Not looking straight at her, he nodded. "I just have to go back in to get the urn."

Taryn brought the car around and looked at the urn as Errol got in. "What are you going to do with her?"

"A long time ago she said she wanted to have her ashes thrown into the wind on the Mediterranean. When I have the chance..." With his hands wrapped securely around the urn, he sat in silence as Taryn drove off.

Though she'd never driven through the streets of Paris, she managed to bring them home with only two wrong turns. She helped Errol out of the car, escorted him to the elevator and pushed the button of his floor.

Once in his apartment, she brought him to the bedroom, undressed him and settled him into bed. He'd put the urn on the bedside table and simply stared at it, saying nothing.

"Do you want me to bring you anything?"

He closed his eyes and shook his head.

148

She put her hand over his, wondering how long it would take him to come out of his stupor.

"*Laisse moi,*" he murmured. Pulling his hand away from hers, he turned away from her and pulled the blankets over his shoulder.

Her meager French, along with his unmistakable body language told her everything; leave me alone.

The following morning she took a taxi to school. After three unanswered knocks at his door, she'd cracked it opened and had received a firm, "Leave me alone."

"What's with Chef King?" Henri asked when she arrived in the class normally given by Errol.

Taryn shrugged. "I don't know. I heard someone in his family died, or something."

Yveline Desperreault, the pursed-lip, middle-aged woman who had taken on the task of teaching Errol's class, looked at Taryn and snapped, "It was his cherished Nana. Of course the boy is distraught." With a cluck of her tongue, she turned to face the class.

The lesson, a review of culinary plating techniques, was long and tedious. Though Madame

Desperreault was reputed to have talent as a chef, her talent for teaching was sorely lacking. She had a droning and draining voice that could turn the most vibrant topic into something bland and blasé.

Taryn was happy to finally be out of the class, out of the school and into her taxi for the ride home. Eager to see how Errol had managed during the day, she put the key in the lock and opened the door.

The apartment was as it had been when she'd left that morning. It was impossible to believe he'd spent the entire day in bed. Worried about the depression he seemed to be in, she tiptoed to his door and pushed it open.

His bed was empty. She glanced toward the closet door. Things had been pulled out and discarded.

"Errol," she called out into the empty apartment. Knowing what she'd find, she went into the bathroom. There were vague signs he'd taken a shower, and some of his toiletries were gone. "Errol."

Hurrying back to his room, she looked for his grandmother's urn. It, too, was gone.

"Damn it, Errol. Where did you go?" she muttered into the room.

The answer, simple and vague, came by way of a hastily scribbled note on the refrigerator door.

Gone for a few days.

Chapter 12

Taryn spent the next four days alone, wondering and worried. Other than the simple note, she had absolutely no idea where he was, what he was doing, or when he'd come home. At school many speculated on his absence: He's mourning in private. He went to the Mediterranean to dispose of his Nana's ashes. He's off partying somewhere to ease the pain.

But the theory that most disturbed Taryn was that he'd returned to a long ago lover; a woman who'd loved Errol dearly and who'd been greatly appreciated by his Nana.

At night she dwelled on that notion, envisioning him wrapped in that woman's arms, his body pressed against hers, and her cries of ecstasy sounding in his ears.

In that endless week, she'd gone through hours of worry, a day of near panic and now two sleepless nights that left her pained and increasingly angry.

Why hadn't he brought her with him? Why hadn't he even bothered to call since leaving? Why had he chosen to go off with this other woman?

Sitting in front of a dinner she didn't have the appetite to eat, Taryn finally allowed the release of a few tears.

She'd been naïve and stupid enough to think she could actually mean something to him. Like so many women before her, she'd misinterpreted all those little kisses, every tender touch, every hushed word in her ear. She'd allowed herself to think they'd meant something.

And in return, she had allowed him to mean something to her. Frustrated with herself and angry at him, she put her hands over her face and let out a pain-filled cry. With her elbows propped up on the table, she sat behind the darkness of her hands, reviewing all that had happened and wondering how she'd let herself get in so deep.

As his playful, flirtatious, wicked ways came back to haunt her, rage slowly simmered up to the top. She opened her eyes and looked around the apartment that was his playpen; the place he brought women to do with as he pleases all while toying carelessly with their hearts.

"Shit!" She grabbed her fork and threw it across the room.

"Is your food really that bad?"

A jolt of relief brought her to her feet. She turned to face Errol and was touched by the loss still visible in his eyes, but his playful grin brought her rage back to consume her.

"I didn't think you'd miss my cooking that much," he said as he set down his bags.

"You really think you can just waltz in and start making cute jokes, Errol?" She heard the venom in her voice. Though surprised, she was happy to discover she was finally ready to stand up for herself.

His eyes immediately hardened as did his tone. "It's my place. I can waltz in and do whatever the hell I want."

She stared at him, angry, hurt, frustrated and lost. "Why didn't you call? Why couldn't you just let me know…?"

"Because it was none of your business."

Her jaw hurt from the pressure of biting down so hard. "Bastard."

He shrugged.

She didn't want to cry… not in front of him. She couldn't let him see… "To hell with you."

"Ah, the little New Yorker finally comes out." He came to stand at the end of the dining table, his gaze condescending and belittling. "I was beginning to wonder if you had any of that New York fight in you."

"If you think I'm going to pick a fight with you, you're wrong. I've had enough of this." She hurried to the sofa, grabbed her purse and headed for the door.

"What, and you're not bringing your things? Old tactic, darling. Every woman who leaves my apartment leaves something behind. Oh, sometimes it's just a memento, something to remember her by, but it's usually an excuse to come back… back to see if they can't get me to change my mind."

She rushed back to her room, shoved a few things in a bag and returned. "I'll come back for the rest when you're not here." Without looking back, she hurried to the door.

"Don't." The condescension had left his voice that'd suddenly reverted to that of the lost little boy.

Her hand on the doorknob, she hesitated and hated herself for it. When he said nothing more, she opened the door.

"Taryn, don't go. Don't leave me alone."

Staring at the carpet in the hall, she murmured, "These past days, all you've been telling me, in every way possible, is to leave you alone."

She heard his steps behind her and knew the tears would flow the moment he touched her.

"I've had plenty of time to be alone." He grasped her by the shoulders and pulled her back into his chest.

Her head fell until her chin rested on her chest. Tears burned their way down her cheeks and dripped off to splash on the floor.

"Please put up with me a little while longer."

"You don't deserve it," she muttered.

156

"I know, but I'm asking you to all the same." He tugged on her shoulders, urging her to return.

For a moment, she held her ground. "Why should I, Errol? You've done nothing but use me when you want and toss me aside when you don't."

"Come." His voice was gentle as he guided her inside and closed the door. "How about some wine?"

She sat on the sofa and nodded as she wiped the tears off her face.

He returned moments later with two glasses and a bottle of red wine. "Truce," he said as he sat beside her and handed her a glass. Keeping one foot on the floor, he leaned back, stretched one leg out behind her on the sofa, and pulled her back to recline on his chest. "How's that for a truce?"

"This does little to explain or excuse how you've treated me."

"Come now, Taryn." He wrapped one arm around her waist. "You've enjoyed it just as much as I have. Don't play so innocent."

He was right and she had little in the way of argument. For a long while they sat in silence, each lost in their own thoughts as they sipped their wine.

When they'd emptied their glasses, Errol poured a little more.

"Nana's name was Simone," he finally said. He almost choked up on the words. "I don't know how old I was when I finally learned that. For the longest time, I really thought her name was Nana."

Smiling wistfully, Taryn nodded.

"Her husband died and left her with seven kids to clothes and feed. For the longest time she'd tell me he'd had a heart attack, but she finally admitted, when I was of age to drink, that he'd gotten into a drunken brawl. He was thrown out of the bar, hit his head and died a few hours after that."

He took a long, slow sip of wine, sighed and remained silent for a while. "Whenever I complained about things being too hard, about not wanting to do a particular chore of something, she'd remind me of all the things she'd had to do. Going to the market, alone, on foot, carrying heavy bags of groceries back. She did all the cooking, cleaning, gardening… she even killed her own chickens."

"Really?" Listening intently, she ran her hand absentmindedly over his.

"And if I ever dared say how much harder life was these days, like when I had to bring firewood in... boy, she'd let me have it. She could spend an hour reminding me how easy I had it compared to when she was a kid."

"Seems like you had a pretty great childhood. Did you resent your parents abandoning you? I mean, maybe it was for the best."

He swirled his glass of wine around, took a swig then swirled it around again. "It took a little while before I finally ended up in Nana's house."

"You said she taught you how to make an omelet at six." Could he really have been abandoned much younger than that?

"I was two, maybe three when my parents ditched me. Talk about the terrible twos."

"Do you remember them?"

"Not really. I mean, I get flashes now and then, but I don't know if it's really my memory or just my imagination. You know, sometimes you just make up stuff, an imaginary world, because the real one sucks so much. Now, when I look back, some of the imaginary stuff almost seems real."

"What happened to you when your parents left?"

He shrugged. "My mom brought me to the babysitter's like usual; she was this nice woman, Carol, who cared for five or six kids in her house. I don't remember much, but I always thought I was her favorite; maybe because I was the youngest. Anyway, one day my mom just never came back to pick me up. At first Carol kept me. The authorities were out looking for my parents, trying to figure out what had happened. I think she thought it was just a temporary thing, you know? Like an accident and my parents would come back in a day or two."

Taryn's heart broke as she listened to him. The pain was evident in his voice. She couldn't imagine being so young and feeling so lost.

"When they finally figured out that my parents were long gone, the authorities took me out of Carol's house. I never found out if she wanted to keep me or not. Either way, I hated having to leave." He fell silent for a while. "During those few days, I tried so hard to be a good boy. I thought that was why my mother left me. I think, somewhere, somehow, I knew.

I knew my life was about to change. I knew something was wrong."

Leaning his head on Taryn's, he gave her a light squeeze and she thought he'd end his story there.

"They sent me to live with this foster mom, a Miss Bender. I don't remember much about her except that I didn't like her. I was always hungry. I was always cold. I was always scared. When a neighbor complained about the little boy left all alone in the front yard, I was taken out of that home and put in another. Things weren't much better. There were a few older kids. The foster parents had a heavy hand when it came to keeping us all in line. When I wasn't getting a beating from the adults I was getting one from the older kids. I think I was there until I was five and a half. I guess the good thing there is that I learned to defend myself. Not very efficiently at first, but it was a good start."

"I never could understand why the authorities leave children with people who have no idea how to raise a child."

He shrugged. "Sometimes it's the parents who are really good actors. They can put on a great show when they have to. Other times it's the authorities who don't do their jobs properly. The last home I went to before finally finding Nana practically had us kids as slaves. They sat around doing nothing but playing video games, drinking and eating while we cooked, cleaned and did everything else they asked us to do. At night, when they were through with us, they put us all in this small dark room; no windows, no beds, no heating."

"It's a wonder you survived at all. How d'you finally find your grandmother?"

"Just after my sixth birthday, I was taken to the hospital. I was helping one of the older kids do the dishes and I'd climbed on the counter to put the dishes away. I fell and broke my arm. Probably the best thing that could have happened. At the hospital a dedicated social worker dug deeper into my family history and finally found Nana. Right out of the hospital I was put on a plane, rode a train for two hours, was in a cab for twenty minutes then in a horse and buggy for another hour."

Taryn sat up and turned to look at him. "A horse and buggy?"

Chuckling, he ran his hand through her hair and leaned in to kiss her. "Nana lived in a small, undisturbed village in northern France. Okay, I'm exaggerating about the horse and buggy, but you get the idea. I mean, it was the kind of place where I had to go out every morning to pump water and stuff. It was rough, but a whole other kind of rough. Nana made me work and sometimes I hated her for it, but I was rewarded for the work I did and now I appreciate all she taught me."

"A lot of character building stuff, huh?"

"Yeah. They say what doesn't kill you makes you stronger. Damn right."

"She taught you how to cook?"

"In a rudimentary sort of way. I mean ingredients were crude and raw, but I learned how to do a lot with little. When I turned sixteen I moved to the city and got a job as a short order cook. A year later I lied my way into the junior chef position on a cruise ship. That led me to the Bronx where I had to literally fight my way into a job. Everything I ever did revolved around cooking, but I knew I didn't just want to be a cook. I wanted more. I tried to get some sort of internship in a big, high class restaurant, but they weren't into that, so I called up the guy I'd worked with on the cruise. He told me the answer to my problem was at the Institute here in Paris, so I worked, saved up some money, and voila... here I am."

"That's quite a journey."

"And, I owe it all to Nana." He gave Taryn a heartfelt squeeze. "I'm sorry I didn't let you in. I'm sorry I didn't bring you with me. It was just something I had to do alone. I wanted to re-immerse myself in the life I'd known with her."

"I understand. I was just worried about you."

"Just worried?" He chuckled softly and kissed her temple. "That didn't look like worry to me."

"Okay, at first I was worried, but after a day or two I got annoyed, then finally tonight... well, I was just plain mad."

"You don't say."

Taryn looked at him, pleased to see the life back in his eyes. Playful mischief had returned to make his eyes sparkle again. "I'm happy you're back."

"So am I."

"Were you really out there alone the whole time?"

He grinned and set his glass of wine on the end table. "You heard about Veronique?"

Taryn tried to shrug off the rumors she'd heard about him and an ex-lover, but she couldn't help the feeling of jealousy that suddenly filled her.

"Veronique lived in the city closest to where my grandmother lived. We knew each other a long, long time ago."

Hating the thought of asking for more information, Taryn waited a moment before turning to look at him.

Errol laughed and kiss her brow. "Veronique moved to Nice five years ago, got married and has twin girls. Does that answer your question?"

He kissed her lips and pulled her in tight. If there were any lingering doubts about where he'd been and who he'd been with, they were all erased as his mouth covered her lips and his tongue twirled around hers in a wet and warm dance. Groaning with pleasure and anticipation, Errol slid his hand into the opening of her shirt, pushed aside her bra, and grabbed her breast.

165

Taryn almost spilled the remains of her glass as her hand lost its ability to hold on. She quickly set it on the table before letting her hand run over Errol's chest. She realized just how much she'd missed his touch these past days. Her body had become accustomed to daily stimulation and now craved the complete satisfaction only he could bring her.

"I missed you," he said between heated kisses.

"Good." She turned to completely face him, kneeling between his legs. With ravaging hands, she pulled apart his shirt, exposing his chest.

His eyes darkened with lust as he licked his lips. "I think my absence has done you some good. Look at how hungry you are."

She couldn't deny it. Her body was obsessed with the thought of touching his. With quick and completely un-romantic moves, she stood and peeled off her clothes then took care of ridding Errol of his.

"You're rushing, honey." Sitting up, his eyes roved over the length of her body as one solitary finger trailed from her nipple to her navel and down to briefly part her lips before dropping to the length of her thigh.

"Yes, okay." She looked pointedly at him. "I want you... now. I'm horny and I want you to fuck me, Errol." She swatted his teasing finger off her thigh. "We can linger over drawn-out foreplay later. Now, I just want..."

He took a rough hold of her hand and pulled her down to straddle him. "You don't have to tell me twice." In one quick motion he was inside her, pushing her down hard over the length of him.

Taryn rode him, fast and furious as her breasts jutted out in his face. His fingers gripped her hips, digging in as he groaned his oncoming release.

"Damn it, woman. It's not going to be over this quick." He pushed her off him and threw her to the floor, pinning her hands high above her head. "You wanted me to fuck you..." He licked her face then trailed down her neck and onward to clamp down on a nipple. As her sigh of ecstasy brushed past him, he drove his erection deep into her.

She thought she'd explode, the sensations were so strong. Was it the week without him? This week of abstinence? Or was it the rough hand he took with her?

"You want me to fuck you, Taryn?" he hissed as he pounded into her, driving her apart with each hard thrust.

"Yes!" Her orgasm swept over her, blocking out anything and everything that could have ever been important in her life. In that moment, under him, with him, fucking him... it was all that mattered.

Chapter 13

If his relationship with Veronique was over and done with, his connection to Xaviera wasn't. Madmoiselle Xaviera Tourneau was tall, with long dark hair that curled stylishly around her face. She had bewitching dark eyes, a sensual mouth and an hourglass figure that was tightly wrapped in a chic black dress that accentuated every attribute.

The moment she saw her, Taryn hated her. And when the woman came to stand close as she spoke to Errol, she hated her even more.

Le Festivale des Arts Culinaires de Paris was the place to see and be seen by the culinary world. As ecstatic as Taryn had been when Errol had invited her, she now stood between Errol and this Xaviera woman seething with what she could only describe as jealousy, not to mention a humbling dose of inadequacy.

"Xaviera, this is Taryn Cummings. She came all the way from New York to attend the Institute."

"*Ah, comme elle est mignonne.*" The plastered ruby red smile on the woman's face said it all. Xaviera was on the prowl, Errol was her target and Taryn was of little consequence. As if Taryn weren't there at all, Xaviera draped her arm through Errol's and looked down at Taryn. "You are a student of Errol's, no?"

Touché, Taryn thought. She was here as his student and assistant, not girlfriend or lover.

Before she could answer, Xaviera turned to Errol. "And here you are, *mon cher Errol*, special guest speaker. You have come a long way, haven't you?"

Errol looked at Taryn. "Xaviera and I studied together a few years ago."

Xaviera leaned suggestively into him, her large breasts pressing against Errol's chest. Her eyes smoldered and her lips pouted with promise. "We did a little more than study, no?"

Taryn saw Henri in the distance and felt a wave of relief. She needed a distraction. She needed to get away from the pair before she ripped the French woman's head off.

"Hey," Henri said. "Fancy meeting you here."

170

Keeping her eyes on Errol and Xaviera, Taryn smiled at Henri. "I'm surprised Err... Uh, Chef King didn't invite the whole class."

"Yeah. I guess he wanted to keep this whole guest speaker thing low key."

Taryn wanted to laugh. Errol was anything but low key. "Seen anything interesting since you got here?"

Errol and Xaviera walked away and Taryn suddenly regretted moving away from them. She wanted desperately to follow them, but knew it would raise too much suspicion from Henri.

But her mind raced with uncomfortable questions. Mainly, what was this woman up to?

"I met the owner of this high end restaurant in the south of France," Henri said. "We talked a bit, exchanged a few ideas, and, well... who knows where it will lead?"

Taryn brought her gaze to him. He was such a sweet young man; good looking in a boyish sort of way. Why in the world hadn't she simply gotten to know him a little better instead of getting all wrapped up in the turmoil that was Errol King?

"The south of France, huh? Sounds amazing."

"Very." He fidgeted a bit and seemed suddenly nervous. "You know, I've really enjoyed working in class with you. Girls sometimes... they don't like to experiment. They don't dare vary a recipe. You're different. You're bold. You like to take chances, do things differently..."

Taryn wanted to argue the point, but had to admit, she'd known many women who didn't change an iota on a recipe, whereas the few guys she'd known who liked to cook were constantly improvising.

"But you," Henri went on, "you are very... how do you say... daredevil in the kitchen. Like the other day when you put olives in your..."

"Oh," Taryn called out suddenly. "Hold on a second." She'd just caught sight of Errol walking out of the building with Xaviera. She hurried to the exit but stopped short of walking out. For a breathless moment she simply stood there, staring at them through the glass doors.

Errol smiled, so charming and beautiful, while his ex-lover drizzled sensuality all over him. Did he have a hard-on right at this moment? Was he imagining all the things he could do to her?

Taryn went pale and her gut jumped to her throat. Could he be imagining all the things he *would* do to her? Was he planning on leaving with this walking-talking sex bomb?

"You okay?" Henri said as he walked up beside her.

Flushed she turned to him. "Yeah. I'm sorry about that. I think I was feeling a little... hot and... I wanted to rush out to get some air, but I'm better now. All's good." She patted him affectionately on the arm and guided him to the auditorium where Errol was set to speak.

"Isn't it another hour before he starts?" Henri asked.

"A little less than that, but I'm tired of standing and want to make sure we have a good seat. After all, he is our teacher and we should be there to support him. I'm surprised the rest of his class isn't here. I mean, even if we weren't invited, they should all know this is going on, and they should want to be here. Well, who knows? Maybe we'll spot some of them later. Maybe when Errol gets up on that stage they'll all come running." Taryn realized the extent of her ramblings and abruptly shut up. Without daring to look his way, she wondered if Henri was aware of what was happening between herself and Errol.

"I wouldn't be surprised," Henri said. "I'm sure they'd all want to know what he has to say. I mean he is one of the greatest chefs in the world."

For the next forty-five minutes they talked about anything and nothing, chatting and telling each other little anecdotes that had brought them where they were. The seats around them slowly filled up and before long a microphone screeched with feedback.

"*Mesdames. Messieurs.. C'est avec grand plaisir que je vous presente, Chef King.*"

Errol was greeted with warm applause as he took to the stage. He looked better than ever and Taryn couldn't believe she had managed to get involved with someone like him. That Chef Errol King, this highly-regarded, sought-after sexy man, was fucking her every night. For all the heartache and turmoil he caused her, she had to admit... there wasn't a dull moment with him. She was aroused just watching him speak, the passion he had for life and cooking making him more and more attractive, along with the commanding strong presence he had onstage. He ruled the stage, and the crowd loved him.

"*Merci. Merci.*" The applause died down and Errol scanned his audience. "*Si je suis ici parmi vous aujourd'hui…*"

Taryn leaned closer to Henri. "I didn't realize he'd be speaking in French the whole time."

"Want me to translate?"

It would be impossible for him to translate everything Errol said. She shrugged. "Give me just the highlights." I'll get the rest from him tonight, she told herself.

At the end of his speech the audience applauded and asked for more, but he humbly bowed and left the stage. Taryn rose to go see him, but quickly noticed that Xaviera had beat her to him.

She finally had to resign herself. With Henri and Xaviera at the festival, Taryn would not have the chance to spend any time with Errol.

"I want to go congratulate him," Henri said as he took a hold of Taryn's arm and led her in the direction of the sexually charged couple.

Taryn wanted to find a way out, but nothing came to mind. Smiling like a dimwit, she stood by Henri as he thanked Errol for the inspiring speech.

"Thank you. I appreciate that, Henri." Errol's gaze swept over the young man than crossed over to Taryn.

She saw the tiniest hint of a question in his eyes and was suddenly happy to have Henri at her side. Checkmate, she thought.

"Let me introduce you to *Mademoiselle Xaviera Tourneau.*"

Taryn wanted to gag. Even on a fresh-faced young country boy like Henri, the woman had an effect. Henri turned beet red and fidgeted horribly as the woman smiled and winked at him.

"*Enchanté,*" Henri finally said as he extended his hand to her.

"*Un plaisir,*" Xaviera returned. She shook his hand, lingering far longer than was necessary. She turned to Errol. "Your students, no?"

176

"Yes," Errol said. "That's right. These are two of my students."

"Have you told them?"

Taryn looked at Errol, trying to keep the horrified sensation she felt down in her gut from showing in her eyes.

"Well, I wanted to keep it as a surprise for Monday, but, hell. Miss Tourneau will be taking over the pastry classes at the Institute for the next three weeks."

Surely she'd gone as white as a sheet, Taryn thought as Errol's words echoed in her head. Next three weeks… this woman would be… in school… around Errol… damn it, no. This woman was a hellcat, a slut. A damned sex goddess, and it was clear she wanted Errol.

Chapter 14

The moment *Mademoiselle Tourneau* stood in front of the class she'd won over every male student and had made an enemy of every girl. Suddenly, students who'd never had the slightest interest in pastry were lining up to take her classes.

Sulking, Taryn moved to the back of the class. She didn't want to be within range of the woman's toxic aura.

"*Bonjour*," she purred. "*Je suis Mademoiselle Xaviera Tourneau.*"

Francois, the hotheaded playboy seated next to Taryn leaned forward to whisper to Henri, "Think we can call her Madame X?"

"*Les pattiseries, ma specialité, sont...*"

Taryn soon lost track as Xaviera went on in quick French. Most of the classes at the Institute were available in English and many were bilingual. Taryn had taken care to avoid the classes given exclusively in French.

Only when a few other girls complained did Xaviera throw in a bit of English.

"*Premièrement*," Xaviera said, then added with a condescending roll of her eyes, "Firstly… *les outils*… the tools of pastry making."

One by one she pulled utensils out of a drawer and showed them to the class, asking students to name the utensil and explain how it was used. After the ever present rolling pin, pastry brush and fluted pastry trimmer, she pulled out what looked like two metal balls, one larger than the other, on the ends of a small wooden handle.

While a few hands flew up to give the answer, Xaviera directed her gaze menacingly at Taryn. "*Quelle est le nom de cet outil?*"

Feeling targeted, her mouth went dry. She'd seen the tool once before, but had no idea what it was called and couldn't remember what it was used for. After a moment of excruciating silence, Taryn finally shook her head. "I don't know."

179

"You don't know?" Xaviera said. Her eyes remained on Taryn, ridiculing her. She held the utensil up for a better look. "You've been taking this class for, how long? Three weeks? Are you telling me that *Monsieur Bouthillier* never brought out such an instrument?"

Monsieur Bouthillier, the teacher who'd introduced them all to pastry making, had never had such a utensil, Taryn wanted to say.

"How do you intend to pass this class if you don't know the basics?" Xaviera went on.

All eyes were on Taryn as she sought to slide under her desk and disappear.

"Where are you from?" Xaviera snapped.

"New York."

Madame X grimaced, shot a disdainful glance at the ceiling and tossed the funny looking tool on her desk. "Well, that explains everything." She crossed her arms in front of her, lifting her bosom until it almost burst out of her top.

Incensed, Taryn balled her fists under her desk, outraged that this woman could treat her in such a way.

"I strongly suggest you learn your way around the kitchen if you want to pass this class." Without bothering to look up at Taryn, Xaviera shot out the unmistakable threat.

Taryn simply nodded while her heart pounded out its fury. There was nothing she could say to the woman who now held the results of this class in her hands.

"Okay," Xaviera finally said with an annoyed cluck of her tongue. "Who then can tell me what this is?"

Henri put his hand up and looked apologetically at Taryn. "I don't remember the name, but it is used to make decorative flower petals and leaves."

"*Bien*," Xaviera said with a pleased nod. "*Très bien*." She shot a victorious glare at Taryn before going on to the next tool.

By the end of the class, Taryn was exhausted. The tension in the class was palpable, or at least it felt that way to her. Did everyone else feel it? she wondered.

After lunch, Taryn headed to Errol's class, but stopped abruptly when she saw Madame X in the room with him. She sat on his desk, her skirt pulled provocatively high on her thigh as Errol sat in his chair looking at her with wicked eyes.

Taryn swallowed the uncomfortable lump in her throat. This was only the first day with Xaviera. How was she going to survive the next three weeks? Not only did the woman deliberately berate her in front of the whole class, but now she was openly going after... After what? Taryn thought. After her man?

Damn it.

She waited until a few other students entered the class before going in to take her seat. Madame X seemed unperturbed by the male audience that now watched her with open interest. If anything, she thrived on it. She leaned toward Errol, exposing her lush breasts to him.

The whole room saw him glanced down at her breasts and Francois dared an envious whistle. It was enough to shake Errol out of his lust-filled gaze and take note of the class. He rose, said a few hushed words to Xaviera who turned and winked at the class before walking out. Her hips swayed an open invitation to all.

She was rewarded with a chorus of appreciative whistles.

Damn the bitch. Taryn wanted to throw something hard and heavy to the back of her head. Instead, she turned her attention to Errol who started the class. She quickly found that she couldn't concentrate on the lesson. Visions of Errol with Madame X continually played in her mind. Her voluptuous breasts. That tiny little waist. Those alluring hips. Damn, the woman had everything to please a man. It was hard to imagine how Errol could resist.

Had they already? Would they?

Would he?

Taryn's newly awakened sexuality felt threatened by this woman who'd obviously been playing the game for a long time. The tricks she must know to please a man.

"Taryn."

The tricks she must have used on Errol, again and again.

"Taryn!"

No doubt Errol would get bored with Taryn's limited knowledge. How long before he succumbed to...?

"The class is over, Taryn. You can go now."

Taryn looked at Errol. The class was empty and Errol stood waiting to leave.

"Are you all right?"

She croaked out an unconvincing, "Yeah," and put her things in her bag.

Errol came to her desk and looked at her, his eyes questioning.

Before he could voice a question, Taryn shrugged. "I'll talk to you about it tonight." She looked pointedly at him. "Will you be home tonight?"

"What a silly question. Of course I'll be home tonight. Where else would I...?" He grinned knowingly.

Feeling flustered, panicked and frustrated, Taryn pulled her bag over her shoulder and pulled her thick technical cooking book to her chest. "I'll see you later," she said as she turned and walked out.

That night she arrived to find Errol already at home.

"You look relieved," he commented.

"A long day. Just happy to finally be home."

"Sorry I couldn't wait around to give you a ride. I knew you had that last, late class and I wanted to get home to try out something new."

"That's okay." She looked at the number of utensils set out on the counter. "What are you doing?"

"I got the strange impression that you weren't very attentive in class today."

"I guess I'm more tired than I thought."

"You were off in space somewhere for the entire class," Errol went on. "I thought I'd give you a quick run-through of today's lesson."

Taryn's gaze swept over the array of cooking implements and noticed the little ball thing Madame X had humiliated her with.

"Today," Errol said. "We took a look at efficiency in the kitchen. Most students learn to cook at home, at their leisure. They take their sweet time; finely chopping an onion, judiciously stirring a sauce, methodically sautéing mushrooms. And, of course,

185

they take an eternity plating the whole damn thing. They have all the time in the world to create, concoct and stage the perfect meal for their friends and family… who, by the way, are never a good judge of true culinary skills.

"In the real world," he went on, "we don't have that luxury. Meals have to be prepared precisely and quickly. That's why as chefs, we need to know our way around a kitchen and have an intimate knowledge of the right tools to use. " He chuckled as he held Taryn's apron up to her, his eyes turning dark and mysterious. "Take off all your clothes, Taryn, and put this on."

Taryn's mouth opened in surprise.

Errol's voice was firm as he said, "Strip for me until you're completely naked except for the apron."

"But…I thought we were going to cook…"

"We are," Errol said, turning the kitchen table around to sit down and face her. "In a way…now strip. I need you naked for this, Taryn."

Taryn unbuttoned her shirt slowly, tossing her shirt onto a chair while Errol watched. She unzipped and peeled down her jeans, leaving her standing in front of Errol in just her lace bra and sheer panties. Her mind still on Madame Xaviera's seductiveness, Taryn suddenly felt inadequate and unattractive in front of Errol.

"Now," Errol said, "take off everything." His voice was firm and commanding, not at all like a lover.

"I don't…" Taryn started saying. She unhooked her bra and was letting it slide off when she covered herself back up.

Errol was in front of her in a swift moment, his hand, pulling her hand off of her bra. "Don't cover up," he said. His lips hover over her ears. "Don't cover up your magnificent breasts, Taryn."

"But they're not so…so…large…voluptuous like…" Taryn dropped her chin to her chest.

"What is it? Something happened in class?"

Errol put his hand to her shoulder.

She shook her head and nodded.

"Yes? No? Maybe?"

The playful tone of his voice was wonderful to hear, but not enough to pull Taryn out of the dark mood she'd allowed herself to slip into. Xaviera was getting to her, in every way possible, and she didn't know how to cope with it. New to this game of love, lust and eroticism, she wasn't equipped to compete with a woman like Xaviera.

Errol turned her to face him. "Why don't you tell me what's really going on?"

The burn of tears stung her eyes as she looked up at him. She clenched her jaw to keep it from trembling, while a ball of hurt crammed her throat.

"It's Xaviera, isn't it?"

She shot him a quizzical gaze. "How d'y...?"

"Xaviera has always had a talent for annihilating any other women in the room... in the building... hell, in the city. What happened?"

Taryn shrugged. "Nothing."

"Come on. I know her. I know you."

"What do you know about her that would make you think she'd specifically target me?"

The playful grin faded and his gaze turned thoughtful and concerned. "You think she specifically targeted you? Only you?"

"I don't think it, Errol. She *did* target *only* me. She was a sweetheart to all the guys in the class and was minimally polite to the other girls... but me?"

"What did she do?"

"She humiliated me in front of the whole class. She taunted me for not knowing…"

"For not knowing what?"

Frowning, Taryn turned to grab the stupid ball thing off the counter. "For not knowing what this damned thing is for."

"Ah, yes." Errol took it from her hand. "This is used to…"

"I know what the thing is for now," Taryn growled.

Setting the instrument back on the counter, he pulled Taryn into his arms. "Don't let her get to you. It's a silly game she enjoys playing. She enjoys the torment of others. If she sees she's getting to you, it'll only get worse. She has that mean-streak in her. One might even call her a bully."

Taryn pulled back to look at him. "Does she know?"

"Know what?"

"About us?"

He shrugged. "I didn't tell her anything, but she probably suspects. She's good at picking up on things like that."

"She wants you, doesn't she?"

He shrugged again. "Could be."

Feeling defeated, Taryn dropped her gaze to the floor. "I can't compete with someone like her."

"Who said anything about competing?"

She met his gaze.

Errol grasped her shoulders, shook her playfully and kissed her brow. "Enough of this for now. I'll pour you a glass of wine, you'll sit back and relax a bit and dinner will be on the table in twenty minutes. How does that sound?"

Taryn sensed there was more to it than just that, but she didn't argue or question. Sitting down with a glass of wine sounded good and she longed to put Madame X out of her mind.

Chapter 15

After a cozy dinner of *pot-au-feu*, Errol and Taryn lingered at the table over a last glass of wine. They'd avoid any conversation that could bring them back to Xaviera, but the question continued to gnaw at Taryn. Was Errol going to have an affair with her? Had it already begun?

"Now feel better?" Errol asked as he rose to clear the dishes.

Taryn nodded slightly before she rose to help him, but he shook his head and gestured to her seat. "Wait here."

A few moments later she felt a strange sensation on the back of her shoulders. "What are…?"

"Close your eyes," Errol ordered. He reached around to unclasp her bra then pulled it off her shoulders.

Once again she felt a strange, but pleasant sensation as something rolled along her back.

"What instrument could possibly create such a sensation on your skin?"

A gentle, probably fluted wheel ran smoothly back and forth. "A pastry trimmer."

"Not bad." He set the tool on the table.

Keeping her eyes closed, she waited a moment.

"Now this."

She felt a gentle but sharp pounding on her back.

"Hurt?"

"Barely."

"Good?"

"Yes."

"What is it?"

"A meat tenderizer."

"Right."

Another moment of silence passed before a sharp scraping sensation passed across her back. "That could be a lot of things. A spatula?"

He passed from shoulder to shoulder. "Feel the width."

She concentrated on the slow passing of the instrument. "A dough scraper?"

"Good." He reached for her hand. "Come on. You've graduated to the next level." He guided her to the couch, but before she sat down, he slowly and meticulously took off every stitch of clothing she had on. Grinning, he said, "The better to help you feel every movement of every tool."

"Right," she said knowingly.

"Lie down and close your eyes."

She did as she was told, then Errol took her hands and set them on the armrest above her head. Moments later she felt a funny prickling sensation across her belly.

"I have no idea," she confessed.

He passed the instrument slowly over one breast, dipped into the valley then up and over the other breast. She nearly opened her eyes, the sensation was so strange and foreign.

"You're not concentrating on what it could be."

"It's funny. It tickles." She concentrated. "This is another pastry thing, isn't it?"

"Could be."

"A roller docker… or dough prickler?"

"Right again." He set it down and quickly brought out the next test.

Three dull blades plied at her skin in unison. "That's easy," she said. "A pastry blender."

"Okay. How 'bout this?"

Two slightly sharper blades rocked back and forth over her thigh. "One of those things you use to chop herbs."

"The name?"

"Oh, something weird and funny."

"Like?"

"Mezzanine?"

"Close."

"Mezza... something."

"You got half of it right. Think of the moon."

"The moon?" She rifled thought her culinary vocabulary. "The moon... lunar? Oh, I know. Mezzaluna!"

"There you go."

Seconds later she felt a vaguely oval pressure on her upper thigh. It cut lightly into her skin, like... a... heart. "A cookie cutter," she said.

"Too easy."

She heard the tinkling of metal against metal as she waited.

"You'll never get this one."

Cold metal touched her breast, surrounding her nipple.

"A guess?" he offered.

"Too vague."

"Here's a hint."

A strangely erotic sensation ran through her as something cool and hard prodded her nipple while the rim of metal remained on her skin. "That's... odd."

"Again?"

She nodded, partly to better discover what the instrument was, but also to feel that sensation again. The prodding motion repeated itself several times.

"I like it," she finally said, "but I can't figure out what it is."

"Want to touch it?"

She brought her hands up, but he pushed them back down. "Not with your hands."

Frowning, she didn't understand where he was going until she felt the cold metal on her lips. She smiled as he gently nudged the instrument into her mouth. Running her tongue along the instrument, she tried to imagine what it looked like.

"Watch your tongue," Errol warned.

The prod that'd aroused her nipple now worked its way to the center of the circular metal rod.

"The only thing I can think of," she said, "is a cherry pitter."

"Ooh, what a talented tongue you have there."

She grinned behind her closed eyes as he set the pitter down and picked something else up. She heard a short, sharp intake of air then a tight suction pulled at the skin of her belly. "Hmmm. That's strange."

"I know you know this one."

She felt nasty and dirty as the thought hit her. Of course she knew what it was... a baster. But she was curious to feel that sucking, suction sensation... elsewhere. "Try again," she whispered.

He knew her too well. In the next instant the suction pulled on an already erect nipple. An excited gasp escaped her and her eyes flew open for the briefest second.

"Oh, you like that one, don't you?"

"You surprised me, that's all." She tried to leave the lust out of her voice, but it still sneaked in.

"Well then, how's this for a surprise." He brought the baster to the sensitive nub of skin between her thighs.

"Oh, shit," she cried out as she brought her hands down.

Errol quickly stopped her from touching the implement and brought her hands back over her head. "Don't make me have to tie you up."

Repeatedly he pushed the air out of the baster and set it on her to suck. "Too much pleasure can get redundant," he finally said as he pulled it away. "We need to find something that will... bring another dimension to your senses. In the meantime, what instrument of the kitchen was able to bring such rapturous cries of pleasure out of you?"

She smiled. "A baster."

"Like a turkey baster?"

She cracked her eyes open and glared at him. "What are you implying?"

He chuckled and put his hand over her eyes. "Never mind. Onto the next..."

A light tickling sensation ran over her wrists. Three times the light touch passed over her skin before Errol lifted her hands and put something under her wrist. Then she felt the unmistakable tug of rope binding her.

"Twine?"

"Yes," he said, his voice suddenly losing its playful appeal. "Ready for that other dimension?"

Taryn hesitated. "Like what?"

In addition to being bound together, Taryn's hands were secured to something that kept her from bringing her hands down in front of her.

"Do you trust me?"

Again, she hesitated.

"Just in case..." Something light and airy brushed across her face.

"A dishcloth?"

"Close."

"Cheesecloth?"

"Perfect." He set the cheesecloth over her eyes and reached under her head to knot it tightly.

"Errol?"

"Trust me," he whispered into her ear. His hand clamped over one ankle and he pulled it up and secured it to the backside of the sofa with another cheesecloth, leaving her feeling vulnerable and over exposed. "Forget everything you hear. Forget everything you've seen. Forget everything you've tasted. Forget everything you can touch. Just feel."

Taryn felt the sharp slap of something rigid yet pliable against her thigh. A surprised yelp escaped her.

"Like I said, too much pleasure can become redundant. Your mind, your body, your skin needs a more intense source of stimulation."

Again the sharp slap on her inner thigh brought out a yelp.

"What implement could cause such delicious pain, Taryn?"

The sharp slap burned across her belly.

"A spatula?" she hissed.

"Too easy." He tossed it aside.

A sound smack reverberated on her upper thigh. Already she could envision the red welt. Swallowing, she wondered how far he would take this.

"What is it, Taryn?" Errol asked as he brought it down again on her forearm.

She winced and brought in a sharp breath. "Something hard. Something inflexible."

"You're thinking too much. Just feel it."

Another smack came to her shoulder. "A wooden spoon," she cried out.

"That's my girl."

"Errol…"

"A little reprieve from the pain, love?"

"Yes."

He rolled something along her leg, starting at her ankle and rolling up to her knee. The implement had ridges or grooves and wasn't quite round as it seemed to deviate from a straight course.

"I don't know," Taryn said.

"Maybe this will help."

He turned the tool upward and Taryn immediately felt its sharp point. Not the sharpness of a knife, but the pointed end of…? She couldn't quite imagine. Several times Errol rolled it from its rounded outer edge to the point and back to the rounded edge again.

"Now?"

She shook her head. "It almost feels heart shaped."

With a light touch, he trailed the point up the inner thigh of the leg that was pulled up to the side of the sofa. Slowly, he introduced the tool to her moistened lips.

"Errol?" Though strongly aroused, she feared his next move.

"Let go and trust me," he whispered. "I wouldn't do anything to hurt you."

He gently nudged the tool in. It was wider, broader, bigger than she'd initially thought. Licking her lips, she surrendered to the odd yet pleasurable sensations the strange tool brought her.

Errol pulled it out, ran it along her lips then returned to push it in a little deep. With a gentle hand he rotated the implement inside her. She felt the workings of the ridges, the ebb and flow of pressure. Still rotating, he repeatedly pushed it in further then brought it out.

Surprised by how much pleasure the strange instrument brought her, she raised her hip to meet it with greater force.

"Don't move," Errol ordered.

Using every ounce of restraint, she remained still, losing herself in the solitary sensation of his tool.

"And if we add this?"

Something warm, moist and gently firm brushed along her lips just outside the rotating ridges inside. Errol's lips and tongue were on her, while he continually plunged into her with the instrument.

"Damn it, Errol," she cried out. She tugged at her wrists as the strength of the intense oncoming orgasm nearly tore her apart.

"Go ahead," Errol whispered. "I want to see."

The brushing motions along her lips quickened as did the spinning inside.

As her orgasm took hold of her entire body, she arched her back, opened her eyes wide under the veil of cheesecloth and let out an inhuman cry.

Chapter 16

"I told you, Taryn," Errol said as he brought four freshly pressed shirts to the open suitcase on the bed. "I have to meet with my producer."

"Last night it was all about teaching me the use of every kitchen utensil imaginable and now you're off to God knows where." She idly spun the lemon reamer he'd used on her the night before between her fingers.

He shot a glance at the tool. "I'd wash that before using it if I were you, and be careful."

Disgruntled, she tossed it on the bed beside her. It landed next to the plastic pastry brush he'd so artfully used along with the reamer. "You never mentioned this meeting before."

"There are a lot of things I don't mention." He grabbed some socks and underwear out of a drawer and dumped them in the suitcase.

"How long will you be gone?"

"Two or three days. Four tops."

"Why can't I go with you?"

He glared at her. "Don't turn into that girl, Taryn."

Pouting, she looked at him. "What girl?"

"Needy and whiny." He shut the suitcase. "Besides, you have schoolwork to keep you busy."

"Does this have anything to do with Xaviera?"

"No."

"She must have been exciting to be with."

He gazed at her. Clearly he wanted to put an end to the conversation.

"I mean, the woman positively oozes eroticism."

"Yes."

"And I'm just…" She let the statement hang in the air, hoping he'd reassure her.

"I'm here with you now, aren't I?"

"Yes, but…"

He snickered and shook his head. "Taryn, Xaviera was a thrill for a minute or so. I'll admit I like things a little wild and kinky, but she brought kinky to a whole other level; a level I had no interest in."

"So, you're not running off to…?"

"You'll see for yourself when you go to school tomorrow and see her in class." He clipped his suitcase shut, picked it up and leaned over to kiss her, entwining his tongue with hers. His free hand grabbed hold of her cheeks and pulled her in closer, his mouth devouring hers.

She kissed him back just as passionately, wanting to show him how much she wanted him, how she should be the only woman for him. She grabbed his hair and tugged him closer to her, kissing him deeply, while her other hand found the front of his pants and slipped inside to grab hold of his hard erection.

She ran her fingers up and down his shaft, circling the tip and pulling on it. She heard Errol groan, "Taryn, where have you been hiding this minx?"

"Shhh…" Taryn said and went down on her knees, unzipped Errol's pants, and pulled out his massive length. What would it be to taste him, to completely devour him? She looked up into Errol's eyes from where she was posed in front of his hard-on, and took him all in while keeping her eyes on his.

He closed his eyes, arching his back, dropping the suitcase to the ground, as he gently pulled Taryn's head closer, guiding her. She took him in with relish, sucking and licking him until he shuddered.

"Taryn," he groaned. "You are the most beautiful and sexiest creature..." He pulled her up and turned her around, pushing her panties down. "You've no need to feel so insecure about yourself." He drove his hard-on deep into her, she buckled forward. His hands gripped her waist, and he plunged into her harder and faster. Within minutes, she cried out her climax while he groaned his shortly after. "No woman," Errol said between breaths, "should feel insecure, if she can make me want to fuck so hard and come so hard like you do."

*****

The next day, he was right. Xaviera was there, all breasts and hips and sultry lips. As she stood at the head of the class watching her students file in, she absentmindedly played with the long chain that dangled between her breasts.

The briefest scathing glance shot at Taryn told her it would be another long and excruciating hour in the presence of Errol's ex.

"Buddy up with me," Henri said when they were given the task of making a trio of pastries.

Trying to avoid looking at Xaviera, Taryn took care of the *petits choux* while Henri worked on the chocolte *éclairs*. Together they made the perfect batch of *mille feuilles.*

"Nervous?" Henri asked when Taryn dropped a wooden spoon for the third time.

Madame X had begun to circulate around the room, taking notes, making comments, tasting, poking and prodding the various pastries. She was headed their way and Taryn anticipated the comments to come.

"*C'est beau,*" she said as she picked up and examined one of Henri's perfect *éclairs*. She picked up the *milles feuilles* and squeezed until the custard spilled out.

Taryn held her breath. What would the witch have to say about her *petit chou?*

"See," Henri said when Xaviera ignored the little pastry and walked on to the next team. "You got all worked up for nothing."

"Yeah," Taryn said with a shrug. "Who knew indifference could be so pleasant."

He grinned and leaned in closer. "You need to cut loose a bit. A few of us are meeting for a few drinks after class. Why don't you come?"

Taryn considered his tempting invitation. Since all her free time was spent with Errol, she hardly knew any of the students in her classes. Going out and getting to know people could do her some good, she thought. Besides, with Errol gone she was all alone in the apartment and it would be a long, dreary night.

The class let out and Taryn sighed her relief. Another day in the presence of Madame X that she could cross off her calendar. After cleaning up and dumping off her apron, she followed Henri out of the Institute. The sun was warm despite the cool chill in the air.

"It's just around the block."

They arrived at the small and intimate establishment, peeked inside and waved their presence to the waiter before choosing a little table set up outside on the sidewalk. Henri ordered a bottle of wine and, while he didn't have Errol's degree of worldliness and finesse, he had a quiet and reserved confidence she liked.

"Where is everyone?" Taryn asked. She peered down the street in the direction they'd come from and couldn't recognize any of the people walking by.

Henri shifted a moment then turned to the waiter who had him taste the first glass of wine. He nodded his acceptance and the waiter bowed his retreat. Henri swirled the ruby red wine around in his glass and grinned.

"They're not coming, are they?" Taryn said.

He shook his head. "Sorry. I should have come straight out and said I wanted to have a drink with you."

Smiling, she raised her glass. "Well, you got me here, and I'm happy to have a drink with you."

"So you forgive my faux pas. I'm not used to this."

She took a sip of wine and nodded. She liked his frank honesty. "To tell you the truth, it's kind of cute. I mean, it's cool that you don't have an established pick up line or two."

Cocking his head to the side, he laughed. "I never was that cool guy who had it easy with the ladies."

"Yet, you're so adorably handsome."

He blushed and Taryn wanted to laugh. He was refreshing in every way.

"You like?" Henri asked as he held up his glass of wine.

Though her knowledge of wine was definitely lacking, she'd recently become accustomed to very fine wines with Errol. She couldn't quite put her finger on it, but there was a lack in depth of flavor that left her a little flat. "It's good," she said all the same. No doubt the bottle had cost a fraction of the price Errol paid, but she was touched by Henri's eagerness to please.

For a few moments they sat in silence, watching passers-by who hurried to run errands, rush to get home, or simply stroll amidst the bistros and shops.

"Is the Institute everything you thought it would be?" Taryn finally asked.

"It's certainly a lot more work than I would have thought, but I'm looking forward to learning to work with ingredients I'm not used to. I think that will be the next lesson. What about you?"

"I've enjoyed every single second so far and..."

"Really? You didn't seem to be enjoying yourself yesterday."

"Ah, yes. Madame X." Taryn shook her head and chuckled. "What a number. It's hard to believe she teaches pastry making when you look at how she fills out a dress. She's probably never eaten anything she's made. I mean, did you see that itsy bitsy tiny waist. I could probably wrap my hands around it."

Henri laughed. "She certainly is... interesting."

"I guess... if you like that sort of thing."

"Don't let her get to you."

"I'm trying." Exasperated by the thought of Xaviera, Taryn felt the temperature rise. She rolled up her sleeves and sought to change the subject. Anything was better than talking about her tormentor.

"How are you coming along on that menu assignment?"

They'd all been asked to create a full six-course dinner. Every course had to be original and creative.

"I'm having trouble with the main course," he admitted. His gaze dipped down to her forearm.

Taryn followed his gaze, saw the red welt and quickly brought her sleeve back down.

Henri reached across the table and slipped his finger under the cuff of her shirt. "I'd always heard the Institute was rough. I knew I'd have a lot of hard work ahead of me and that it wouldn't be easy. I'd also heard of the tyrant Chef King could be at times."

Casting her gaze aside, Taryn swallowed. "Easy and permissive teachers only breed mediocrity."

"I've also heard a lot about Mr. Kings personal preferences," Henri went on. "He likes things rough."

Taryn said nothing as she picked up her glass and took a sip.

"He gets pleasure out of bringing pain..."

"I thought you wanted to have a drink to discuss school, cooking, anything other than a teacher's personal life." While her defenses had gone up on the inside, she managed to speak with surprising calm and poise. The words almost sounded light and amused as they floated in the air.

"Taryn, I just think you should know…"

She pulled her hand away and pressed her lips tightly together.

"If he's already playing this rough with you, don't think it'll get easier. He'll want it rougher and more brutal. It's no secret what he'll…"

She cocked an annoyed brow and immediately regretted it. She knew he meant well. "Look, Henri, I'm a big girl. Don't worry about me. After all, I'm a New Yorker. I know rough."

"Fine, but I think you should know one last thing about Chef King. His lovers never last longer than a month or two. It's already been how long for you?"

Her mind and body went numb as his words sank in. She wanted to argue, to tell him he had no idea what he was talking about. But it made so much sense. How much longer could they go on like this? How much longer before he grew bored of her?

How long before he went off looking for a new toy?

Chapter 17

Taryn sat in the passenger seat of Henri's car, taking in the beauty of the lush countryside far outside Paris. They'd already been driving for almost four hours and she still gasped with awe as the beauty took her breath away.

After a third day home alone, she'd finally accepted Henri's invitation to visit a dairy farm in the rolling hills of the region of Alsace.

"Knowing where real food comes from is important," he'd argued. "I also know this organic farmer I think you'd like to meet. And I took down the address of a pigeon farmer."

She shook her head and grimaced. "I still have a hard time wrapping my head around the idea of killing and cooking a pigeon."

Henri shrugged. "No different than killing or cooking a chicken."

Pressing a tight grin, she looked at him. "Thanks."

"For what? Introducing you to a pigeon farmer."

"For insisting I come with you. This is nice. I never thought the countryside could be so spectacularly beautiful."

He looked out at the pastures, meadows and gentle valleys that surrounded them. "It is pretty, isn't it? If we have time, we'll stop at a vineyard. Alsace has great white wines."

They stopped briefly at the pigeon farm, but Taryn still found herself unable to digest the idea of eating pigeon.

"I know I have to keep an open mind about these things," Taryn said as she got back in the car. "But to actually see them in those cages…"

Henri chuckled and drove off. After skirting the city of Haguenau, Taryn noted a subtle difference in the signs that dotted the roadside. Her French was weak, but she had a good idea of what a French word should look like.

"Is it just me, or have we left France?"

Laughing, Henri playfully slapped her thigh. "If we leave the country, believe me, I'll be the first to let you know."

"Then what's with all these... Are those Dutch names? I mean Vosges and Betschdorf. That's not French."

"You're very perceptive, but that's not Dutch. It's German." He turned the car in the direction of Walbourg. "We're very close to the French/German border."

Their next stop was a dairy farm. Owned by *Monsieur Chartrand*, the farm was set in the middle of some of the most beautiful countryside Taryn had ever seen. The rustic farmhouse was inviting in an old world way, and picture perfect. Everything about the look and feel of the farm spoke of old times, old customs, and old ways.

Inside the graying old barn, however, the old looking country farm was a marvel of modern technology. While milking was occasionally done by hand to show visitors how it was once done, a lot of modern machinery now surrounded the process of getting milk from a cow.

"I can't believe the cows aren't freaked out by those pump things attached to them."

The farmer, a middle-aged man with a sun dried face and calloused hands, looked at her. *"Dey like de pumps,"* he said in a heavily accented English.

Henri patted the bovine between her big, brown eyes. *"Est-ce que je peux prendre la cariole pour aller au ruisseau, Monsieur Chartrand?"*

"Bien oui, bien oui."

Taryn looked at Henri for a translation.

He took a hold of her arm and led her out of the barn and into the stable. "If you think the scenery was beautiful on the way here, wait until you see this." All while murmuring gently to the horse, he led it out of its stall and deftly hitched it to a small wagon.

"Where are you taking me?"

Grinning, he helped her up onto the wagon seat and pulled himself up beside her. With a quick but gentle flick of the reigns, he set the horse in motion. "I love that smell, don't you?"

Taryn sniffed the air and glanced sidelong at him. "Really? It smells a bit like manure."

He shook his head. "Beyond that."

The horse trotted at a brisk pace along a dirt path that led away from the barn and farmhouse. Soon the odor of manure diminished and left room for fresh country air.

"Ah," Taryn said with wonder. She'd smelled fresh laundry before and had often sniffed air deodorized with artificial scents, but nothing compared to this. "That smell. Yes. That's…"

"Pure. Refreshing. There's nothing like real country air. Breathe it in. Fill your lungs. Feel it flow through your nostrils."

She giggled. "You really like it out here, don't you?"

"Nothing better." He glanced at her. "Don't get me wrong. I love Paris, but my heart…" He pounded at his chest with his fist. "My heart is out here."

Pastures of green seemed to go on for miles and miles. "Are we still on Monsieur Chartrand's land?"

They crested a small hill and Henri pulled the horse to a stop. "You see that creek down there?"

Taryn looked down, but Henri guided her gaze further out. "Way out over there."

The hills rolled on and on, lazy and lush with only the dirt path cutting through it like a dusty dull ribbon. In the distance, Taryn spotted the sparkling reflection of water gurgling its way down the creek.

"Yeah, I can see it."

"Monsieur Chartrand's land ends at that creek. It curves over there." He pointed to their right. "And over there, his property ends with that forest."

"Wow. That must feed a lot of cows."

He grinned and nudged the horse on. "Have you ever been to the country before?"

She turned to him. "Does Cape Cod count?"

With a charming chuckle, he shrugged. "I don't know Cape Cod."

Taryn shook her head. "No, Henri. I've never really been to the country. I've lived in New York my whole life. We went to the beach in Jersey a few times, went out to the mountains in the Catskills, but I've certainly never been on a farm before."

He reached for her hand. "Then I'm happy to be the first to introduce you."

Laughing, she leaned playfully into him. He was so easy to be around; so uncomplicated. There was never a dark cloud of moodiness that threatened to erupt; never a streak of anger bubbling over. It was nice being with him; safe.

As they made their way down to the creek, Taryn let the rocking motion of the wagon lull her into a deeply relaxed state. The stress of the past week faded and bliss caressed her like a warm summer breeze. When the wagon suddenly stopped, she took in the sight Henri had wanted to surprise her with.

The creek of pure, clear water splashed over large stones then fell in gentle cascades. A large apple tree grew on the very edge of the creek, offering the only hope of shade. Beyond it, a field of corn rose high, blocking their view to the right offered a sense of intimacy.

"I thought this might be a nice change of pace from the days at the Institute," Henri said. "I've always loved this particular spot. After the immensity of endless fields, this little nook…"

"I see what you mean." Taryn hopped off and looked around. A pair of cardinals fluttered around, chasing each other in their own little ritual dance.

"This is heaven." Taryn turned to see Henri reach for a basket in the wagon.

Blushing, he held it up. "Lunch for two."

He was so sweet. Taryn knew he wanted to please her, but began to wonder what had really brought him to invite her on this trip. Keeping a platonic grin on her lips, she helped him set a blanket on the ground then sat and watched him as he pulled a variety of items out of the basket.

"You brought enough to feed an army," she said.

"Just because we're out of the city doesn't mean we can't eat well."

"Let's see," she said as she picked up each item he set down. "The French cheeses; *Brie de Meaux, Camembert de Normandie*, and… *Munster Géromé*? But Munster isn't French."

He grinned. "Again, very perceptive. Munster is a city in Germany where it is said the monks there once made this cheese. However Munster is also Latin for monastery and some say Irish monks settled here and made the cheese. Either way, it is a cheese that is made in this region."

"Oh, that's cool." She continued her itemizing. "Pears, apples, and green and red grapes; refreshing to the palate. *Paté de foie gras, terrine de sanglier* and *confit de dinde*; all sounds good. A baguette; of course. A bottle of fine wine from Alsace… wow, let me try to pronounce this one; Gewurztraminer."

"Close. It's pronounced gah-vorts-trah-meener."

"Well, we can't have a picnic without that, right? And, for dessert, *profiteroles*. Wow, you went all out."

"Think I forgot anything?"

"Coffee?"

Grinning, he pulled out a thermos.

"I was only kidding," Taryn said with a hoot of laughter.

"Just in case you need a caffeine boost after all this food."

While Taryn cut off a chunk of soft camembert, Henri opened the bottle of wine and poured two glasses. "Here," he said as he opened the brie. "Try this." With a spoon he carved out a small piece, squished it into the spoon with a fork then poured a sip of wine over it.

Taryn opened her mouth as he guided the spoon to her, feeding her. The soft cheese and Chardonnay blended perfectly over her tongue. She tore off a piece of the baguette and stuffed it in her mouth over the cheese and wine. "It's like a Swiss fondue in my mouth." Her muffled voice was filled with laughter. "This is really good."

They settled in to taste the various cheeses and patés while taking in the beauty of their surroundings.

"You know," Taryn said as she glanced at Henri. Her belly was already stuffed with bread and paté, but she enjoyed the big, juicy grapes with tiny bites of cheese. "When you invited me out here, I thought you were going to take me to your farm."

He nodded. "So did I."

"Is Monsieur Chartrand your father and you didn't want to tell me?"

Laughing, he reached for another fistful of baguette, but seemed to have no interest in eating it. "No. My father's not quite that old." Leaning into her, he put his cheek to hers and pointed far down the green hills to their left. "My farm... my family is over there."

She turned to him. "But we're so close. Why...?"

"I was afraid... if I brought you to my home... to meet my parents, you'd... I didn't want to scare you off by being too... presumptuous."

Smiling, she looked into his eyes. "You really are an old fashioned guy, aren't you?"

"I was raised in an old fashioned way, by old fashioned parents in an old fashioned part of the country. What can I say?"

"I think it's sweet, but I wouldn't have thought any less of you because you introduced me to your parents, Henri. I mean, we're friends; practically co-workers in a way."

Chuckling, he looked down at the picnic blanket then slowly brought his gaze back to her. "I guess I'd hoped..." His voice was a soft whisper. "I enjoy working with you. You're easy to talk to, and you make me laugh." His fingers found her cheeks and chin. "So beautiful..."

He leaned in and kissed her; his lips tender and questioning.

For a brief moment, Taryn leaned into the kiss. His lips were soft and the kiss so innocent and pure. It lacked the harsh demands and high expectations she'd become used to. Warmed by the whole atmosphere that surrounded her, by his sweet touch, she surrendered to the kiss, but quickly pulled back. "Henri," she mumbled as she brought her fingers to her lips. "I'm sorry, I can't."

Henri frowned. "It's Chef King, isn't it?"

Taryn shook her head. "No…"

"Then what is it?" Henri asked. "We're in the middle of the most romantic place in the world…"

Taryn silenced him with her finger to his lips. "I…"

Henri looked earnestly at Taryn, his eyes filled with longing. He took her finger into his mouth and sucked on it and closed his eyes. "You taste as sweet as you are." He kissed her fingertips. "I would be good to you, I would treat you as the lady you are, I would…Chef King would only hurt you, Taryn."

226

"Henri…" Taryn tried again. As much as she wanted to forget Errol King, as much as she wanted to break from him and have a normal relationship with a man she could call a boyfriend, she couldn't stop wanting him.

Chapter 18

After the aborted kiss, Henri drove Taryn down to his own family farm. His parents, Gilles and Yvette, were kind and inviting, while Henri's younger brothers, Pierre and Bertrand, were curious and intrigued.

"*Elle est joli,*" Bertrand said as he shyly glanced up at Taryn.

"Of course she is beautiful," Henri said as he patted his younger sibling on the head.

They all had dinner together and Taryn was charmed by them all. The atmosphere was light and cheerful; the food plentiful and full of flavor.

"I see where Henri gets his culinary talent," Taryn said.

Accompanied with a robust red wine, the dinner hour was filled with tales of Henri's childhood, anecdotes of farm life and a few colorful fibs from the two younger boys. After dinner, Yvette showed Taryn the room she'd sleep in.

"I hadn't really thought we'd be staying overnight," Taryn told Henri after his mother left them. She looked around the small, but cozy room. "I didn't even bring anything."

"I'm sorry. I should have mentioned how far away from Paris this was." He looked down at the floor. "I guess I thought you'd choose not to come if I told you we'd be going five hours from Paris."

"Don't worry. I don't mind. It's nice out here. I like the change of pace."

He nodded. "Let me know if you need anything."

Taryn closed the door and looked around. Henri's mother had already set some flannel pajamas on the bed along with a pair of warm, fuzzy slippers. "A real change of pace," Taryn whispered as she ran her hand over the flannel.

Her phone rang and she sat on the edge of the bed to take the call, her hand still absentmindedly running over the flannel. "Hello."

"Taryn," Errol snapped. "Where are you? I've been calling the apartment for an hour."

"Errol, I'm so happy you called. It's been such a lovely day and I wanted to share it with you. And tell me, how's your meeting going?"

"We've begun shooting my television show and everything is running smoothly. Now answer me. Where are you?"

"I'm out in the country learning all about dairy farming, pigeons, vineyards and organic farming. It's been a beautiful day and so fascinating. The air is wonderful out here."

"The country?"

She could almost hear the disdain in his voice.

"Yes. The region of Alsace."

"Alsace? Why the hell did you go all the way out there? There are plenty of farms close to Paris."

"I wasn't doing the driving. Henri brought me out here." After a long silence, Taryn said, "Errol? Are you still there?"

"You went out to the country with that... hick?"

"Errol, don't say that. Henri's been perfectly sweet and charming. He's been a great guide. And you know, he knows a lot more about food and cooking than you give him credit for."

"Yeah, I bet he does."

Amused by this unexpected jealous side of him, Taryn chuckled. "Errol."

"I honestly don't see what's so funny, Taryn. If you wanted to go out to the damn countryside, you should have told me. I would have brought you to some of the finest, most beautiful…"

He stopped and Taryn could hear his exasperated breaths.

"And where are you now?"

She hesitated.

"Taryn, where are you? I know you're not at home. I just called there. Where are you staying tonight?"

"We stopped for dinner at his parents' house. It's too late to drive back to Paris, so…"

"No."

"What do you mean, no?"

"I won't have it. I won't have you sleeping out in some country shack with that…"

"Errol, you're being ridiculous." Her amusement faded as she saw just how unreasonable he was. "It's a perfectly beautiful home and they've been so welcoming. His mother even laid out a pair of pajamas for me."

"How quaint."

"I have my own room, if that's what you're…"

"Taryn, I want you home, in my apartment, in my bed."

"But you're not even there."

"All the more reason!"

"Errol, it's late. It's already growing dark outside. Besides, there are a few more farms Henri would like to visit tomorrow."

"I don't care, Taryn," Errol snarled. "If you want to go out and visit farms, I'll take you out to visit farms. Do you understand me?"

Taryn inhaled deeply as she considered his demand. "Errol," she whispered as she let the air slowly seep out of her lungs. "I don't understand. What are you afraid of?"

He groaned and for a moment she thought he'd hang up on her.

"Do you really think I haven't noticed, Taryn?"

"Noticed what?"

"The way he looks at you; those puppy dog eyes... all country charm and boyish lust."

"I think you're exaggerating."

"Really. Are you going to tell me that he hasn't made a single move on you since you've been out there? That he hasn't held your hand? Wrapped his arm around your shoulder? Kissed you?"

Taryn remained silent. If she told him...

"You don't have to say anything, Taryn. Your silence is more than enough."

"Errol," she hushed. "It was a brief and innocent kiss. I told him right away I had no intention of..."

"It doesn't matter what your intentions are. Don't you get that? If he has intentions, he'll do anything to change your mind. He'll do anything to make you think he's the better... I bet he's already badmouthed me, hasn't he?"

Silence.

"Hasn't he!?"

Chapter 19

Errol tossed his phone onto the couch of his dressing room and raked his fingers angrily through his hair. Pacing the room, he considered his options. They'd already taped more shows than they'd originally planned.

But leaving now to go... where? He grabbed his phone and scrolled through his files to find all the information he had on each student.

"Henri," he muttered as he came to the young farmer's name. "In Walbourg."

With the snap decision made, he grabbed his jacket and walked out.

"Errol," his producer called. "I wanted to go over the last bit that you did. I think the lighting was all wrong and that thing... what was that... cow's brain? A *riz de veau*?   Hey, hold on. Where you going?"

"Sorry, Danny. I've got urgent business back home."

"But, we have a show to do. Everybody's here, waiting and ready. And all the food we…"

"Personal emergency. I have to get there."

"Hey," Errol's agent said as he came up to him. "Errol, buddy, a lot of money has been put into this production. You can't just up and leave when…"

"We got more shows in the can than you'd planned. You know damn well you'll get all that money back and more, so save the lecture."

"Getting all of this together wasn't easy, you know."

"Don't give me a hard time. I have to get home. That's all."

An hour later he was on a flight home. He slept as much as he could on the flight, though his sleep was constantly disturbed by dreams of Taryn.

The thought of her in another man's arms… it was enough to drive him mad. What was she doing, right then, at that very moment? Was she with Henri?

With that young juvenile? Naked in his bed, against his hard, young body? Was he touching her soft skin? Kissing her elegant neck? Watching those beautiful eyes of hers close in ecstasy as he thrust into her?

In a fit of rage, he got out of his seat, waking the other passengers around him. He muttered an insincere apology and paced up and down the aisle until the flight attendant told him to sit down and buckle up.

Moments later they landed at Charles-de-Gaulle airport, where he quickly made arrangements for a flight to Strasbourg. There, he rented a car and sped his way to Walbourg. His hands gripped the steering wheel with fiery rage as he imagined Taryn waking in Henri's arms that morning.

Had they made love all night? Had that damned young country virgin tried to please Taryn the way only a real man could? Was he, at this moment, still holding her in his arms, kissing her, arousing her, fucking her?

With Henri's address permanently engraved in his mind, Errol drove through the beautiful valleys of the Vosges Mountains without even noticing them.

The beauty of his surroundings was lost on him as he thought only of Taryn and the night she'd spent with her novice lover.

He pulled up in front of the little, old country house and wanted to gag. It was so stereotypically quaint, he thought he'd vomit. Instinctively, his gaze swept over the windows of the second level. Which room was hers? Better yet, which room was Henri's?

Just as an older man walked out of the house and came to greet him, Errol got out of the car and walked up the path to the house.

"*Bonjour*," the man said with a jovial grin plastered to his ruddy face.

"Taryn," was all Errol said.

The jovial grin faded and the older man turned back to the house. Moment's later Taryn emerged with her lovelorn puppy nipping at her heels.

"Errol. My God, what are you doing here?" Though clearly surprised and shocked, she smiled as she came up to him.

Errol nodded a menacing greeting at Henri. "Get in the car, Taryn."

"You must have traveled many hours to come out here," Henri said. "Why don't you come in for breakfast?"

"I ate on the plane."

"Errol," Taryn said, her face bright and glowing with effervescence and joy. "Henri and I were just talking about going up to visit Chateau…" She looked back at Henri with a befuddled and amused grin. "Fleckenstein, right?"

Henri nodded. "You could join us. It's a beautiful…"

"I have no desire to visit anything whatsoever with you," Errol said.

Smiling an annoying amount of glee, Taryn came up to him and put her hand to his arm. "There are a few farms we want to see along the way. Henri's parents say the castle is lovely this time of year and we could…"

"No," he grunted.

Her smile faded and she reddened as she glanced at Henri then looked at Errol. "There's no need to…"

"Get in the car."

"Errol."

"Taryn, just get in the damn car."

"Hey," Henri said as he took a step forward.

"Stay out of this, son. I'm taking her home." Errol grabbed Taryn's wrist, turned on his heel and dragged her out to the car.

Looking over her shoulder she waved. "It's all right, Henri. Thanks for everything. Please, thank your parents for me. I had a great time."

"Get in the car." Errol opened the door and shoved her inside then slammed the door behind her.

"What's gotten into you?"

Staring straight ahead, Errol drove off, leaving a cloud of dust to blot out the image of Henri who stood, stunned, as he watched the car drive away.

"Errol. What is with you? I was just."

"I told you I wouldn't stand you staying here."

"You're blowing this all out of proportion. Henri is a classmate and he's helping me get familiar with…"

"I don't want to hear it."

"For crying out loud, Errol. You can't keep me from going where I want. I'm not your property to do with as you will."

"You became mine the moment you made my home yours, you got that?"

"That's what you think."

"Damn it, Taryn." He suddenly slammed on the brakes and turned onto a narrow dirt road that cut through a corn field.

"What the hell are you doing?"

Errol shut the motor and pounced on her. In an instant, his hands and lips were all over her, devouring her, tasting her, licking her. At first she resisted, and tried to push him off as she clenched her jaw tight to keep him from entering her mouth.

"Tell me what you did with him."

"What?"

"That country bumpkin… that hick."

"Nothing."

"Did he touch you?" He tore open her shirt and unclipped her bra. Angry and possessive, he grabbed her breasts. "Did he touch you, Taryn? Did he slip his hand in to feel you up?"

"No."

He unfastened her jeans and shoved his hand down her front until his fingers circled her sensitive nub. "Did he?"

"Errol, no."

Clasping his mouth over a nipple, he suckled then sank his teeth in.

"Ouch, Errol. You're hurting me."

Sitting back, he looked into her eyes. "You don't know what hurt is." He got out of the car and came around to open her door. With a firm grasp on her wrist, he yanked her out of the car, slammed the door shut and pushed her up against the car.

With an urgency that consumed him, he pressed his body against hers and rammed her mouth with his tongue. His hands kept busy tearing off her clothes and throwing each item to the ground.

"Errol, what are you…?" Taryn's voice was filled with the thrill of the unknown and the fear that accompanied it.

Errol kicked off his shoes and pulled off his pants. "I'm showing you who you belong to; who you belong with. I'll not have you going off with another man, Taryn." He pushed down his jeans and plunged his long harden anger deep inside her, and she moaned in response before she began swerving her hips in response, rocking with his rhythm. It was exactly what her body craved. She clenched while Errol, with relentless intent, pounded into her.

"Oh Errol!" she moaned, clawing into his back. He was so hard and large, she'd never felt so full. "I want you, more of you, please...harder. Take me harder so I know you're real, back into my life, and not just a dream."

"I'm not in your dreams, Taryn," Errol pounded hard. "I'm very much real, as my fucking you now is real. You're mine," he repeated with every hard thrust. "Mine."

Quickly, too quickly, he spilled all his anger, jealousy and insecurities into her. Sweaty and breathless, he leaned into her and brushed his lips across her ear, taking her hand and lacing his fingers through hers. "You're mine."

Chapter 20

As Taryn dressed for her first night at home with Errol, she smiled as she replayed their hour long frolic in the cornfields of Alsace. At first, she was worried about the possibility of being seen by strangers. She was naked and doing unspeakable things with this man out in the open. What would French country folk think?

But after Errol quickly spent himself, he took her again, slowly, deliciously and with the tender hands of a man who treasured his woman. Through his kisses, he'd confessed his sins. "I knew the moment I saw your photo, I wanted you, Taryn. I knew I wanted to be the first to discover you. Why do you think I planned to meet you before you met the rest of the class? Damn it, I knew all the young men in class would do all they could to get your attention, to impress you."

She'd looked at him with shock. Had he really gone to all that trouble? Did he really wanted her that much? As he made love to her, with his eyes filled with lust and his lips soft as they caressed her skin, she couldn't imagine herself with any other man but him.

"I loathe the notion that you enjoyed yourself with that young Henri. No other man should hear you laugh the way I do. No other man should please you the way I do. No other man should touch you. I'm the only man, Taryn." His lovemaking had become more ardent. "I'm the only man, do you understand me?"

A worrisome voice called from the back of her consciousness, warning her of the danger of such obsessive behavior; all this possessiveness and jealousy. It was flattering to think he wanted her all to himself, but it was also troublesome to see the extent of his obsession. She nonetheless chose to ignore it. This man, as beautiful, charming and talented as he was; this man that so many women would go to the ends of the earth to get within arms-length of... he wanted her. He wanted her, cared for her... He wanted to possess her. And she felt the same for him.

"I love you, Errol." The words had snuck out of her mouth of their own volition.

Again, as she looked at the tantalizing lace costume Errol had insisted she wear, she blushed as she remembered uttering those dangerous words. Her breath had caught in her throat as she'd anticipated Errol's sardonic laughter, but it never came.

Instead, he'd replied with a request. "You love me, Taryn?" he'd said as his hands gripped her buttocks and squeezed while his erection sought out her deepest desires. He thrust into her, causing her to groan. "I don't believe you. I don't believe anyone who says that. What would you do to prove it?"

"Anything."

"Anything?"

She'd known instinctively what he'd wanted from her. She'd do anything to show him the depths of how she felt, this poor man, this man who had never felt love from anyone except the nana he recently lost. Despite his tough exterior, his dominating personality that made him rule the kitchen as well as the bedroom, he was a caring, deeply passionate and sensitive man. She saw that part of him, even when she wasn't looking, when he took care of her after she had food poisoning. She saw that every night when he made love to her, the tenderness he would have for her when he bathed her, took care of her, made sure she ate, slept, and did well in her studies. It hurt that he didn't think he could ever be loved, that he could never experience that, but she knew she loved him...this complicated deeply flawed beautiful man, and she had to try.

For weeks he'd hinted at his interest in seeing her bound; handcuffed. They'd briefly sampled the effects of being tied up the first time they'd made love, and it seemed to ignite his desire to see more. However, the thought of such complete lack of control unnerved Taryn and her fear had kept her from allowing him to fulfill this fantasy with her.

Now, with their emotions so clearly spelled out, she'd succumbed to his wishes; in part to please him, to prove to him how much he meant to her, but also to satisfy her own curiosity.

What would he do with her once she was handcuffed?

Shy, despite the many degrees of nudity in which he'd already seen her, she silently emerged from the bedroom. While the black lace traced its way across her belly, it circled her breasts, leaving them entirely exposed. The crotchless panties added only a trim of frilly lace about her thighs and above her buttocks.

"Why the blush on your cheeks?" Errol said as he turned and took in the sight of her. He reached out for her hand and led her to the dining room. "Let's see what I have planned for dinner tonight. Since we've been apart for so many nights, I want this night to be something special; something you'll remember."

Taryn looked at the assortment of jars and bottles set on the table. "Looks like you're ready to make a sundae," she said as she picked up a bottle of chocolate syrup and a jar of cherries. Also on the table were a pot of honey, a container of whipped cream, a jar of marmalade and a bottle of Grand Marnier.

"I think we'll start with a blind taste test," he said. He pulled two sets of handcuffs from his back pockets.

Taryn swallowed the ball of uncertainty that quickly rose to the back of her throat. "Funny," she said with a nervous chuckle. "I thought you were going to pull out a blindfold."

"In due time." He held the handcuffs out, letting them dangle in front of her. "Ready?"

Putting on a brave face, she smiled and held out one wrist. "You do have the keys, right?"

"You worry too much, dear." He clamped the handcuff to her wrist then guided her down to the floor so he could clamp the other cuff to the table leg.

She looked at the big table, its solid oak legs sturdy and strong. She'd secretly hoped he'd handcuff her to something she had a chance of freeing herself. As she lay back, she stared up at the underside of the tabletop. Errol clamped the other handcuff to her wrist and stretched her arm out to clamp it down to the other table leg.

"Comfortable?"

Her breathing was a little more rapid than it'd been just moments earlier. She nodded.

"Good girl." Errol ran his fingers through the palms of her hands, down along the length of her arms, brushed against her breasts and into the valley of her waist, over the swell of her hips and down her legs to her ankles. Kneeling at her feet, he pulled a handkerchief from his pocket. "Let's see what you really know about cooking ingredients." He leaned over her and bound her eyes.

"I'm not sure I like this."

"You will."

Through the darkness of her blindfold, she heard a jar scrape along the top of the table. "Now, don't bite," he said as he brought his finger to her lips.

She licked his finger and immediately recognized the taste of blueberry jelly. Instead of calling out her answer, she licked his finger clean, taking the time to slowly run her tongue along the length of the digit.

"If you continue like that, we won't make it to the third ingredient." He pulled his finger away and sought another ingredient.

"That was blueberry jelly," she said.

"Right. Now open wide."

She reluctantly parted her lips and felt a few cool drops of liquid drip into her mouth. Having seen only sweet ingredients on the table, she was surprised and grimaced. "Ah, lemon juice?"

"Yes." He popped open another jar. "Now you're really going to have to open wide."

Again, she just barely parted her lips.

"You want to play it that way?" He pressed something cool and bitter to her lips, parting them further.

Bitter, salty, tangy… she knew it had to be something that was marinated. As he slipped the ingredient further into her mouth, she realized how big it was… a pickle. Slowly he drove it to the back of her throat before gently pulling it back out.

"You like that, don't you?"

Nodding, she slipped her tongue out and ran it along the pickle.

"I'm starting to get jealous."

He pulled the pickle away and stood. Taryn heard the sound of fabric brushing against fabric then the clink of a belt buckle as it hit the floor. Errol opened another jar, then straddled her. She felt his skin against hers as his legs brushed against her hips.

Slowly he crawled up until his knees were up to her arms. She knew what he was up to and anticipated his next move. The softness of his skin dipped in chocolate syrup brushed lightly against her lips. It could have been his finger, but she knew better. It was a part of him that she had come to crave in her in every way.

After only a quick lick of the chocolate, she said, "Chocolate."

"Sure? Taste again." He gently nudged his way into her mouth and she felt his budding arousal grow even harder while she sucked and teased him with her tongue.

Pleased by his reaction, she licked all the chocolate off him, slowly until he was groaning. Then she continued sucking, taking him deep to the back of her throat.

"God, Taryn," Errol groaned. He began thrust slowly against her while she licked and sucked harder, enjoying the delicious taste of him filling her. He was a man through and through, and she appreciated and loved every part of him. Feeling him grow harder until he was like hard candy, she sucked in and out faster and faster until he had to pull out.

"Okay," he said between clenched teeth, "if you don't stop, we won't be able to get to the other items I have planned," as he pulled back and got off her. "We're jumping the gun a bit here."

He opened another jar, but instead of bringing it to her lips, he slathered the sticky liquid over her breasts. As he brought his lips over her breasts to lick her clean, his tongue circling her nipples over and over again until they were hard enough for him to suck on and kiss. He brought his mouth up to hers and kissed her, entwining his tongue with hers until she can taste the sweet honey that he had licked off of her breasts. Honey never tasted as sweet as when it came from his tongue. She sucked hard on his tongue, wanting more of him, wanting to taste the honey all over him. He brought his lips to kiss her nose and brow as he pulled the blindfold off her eyes.

She watched him, amazed by his hunger and thrilled by his desire to touch her, taste her, devour her. She'd never seen him so enraptured, nor his hard naked body more magnificently aroused.

When he'd licked her clean, he pulled back and looked at her, his eyes hooded and wicked. He grabbed her ankles and pulled her legs apart then lifted them straight up into the air. Licking his lips he looked down at the opening of her crotchless panties.

"We'll see how flexible you are, my young goddess." He pushed her legs up toward her head until he was able to slip each foot under the lip of the table.

Though increasingly aroused, she felt nonetheless vulnerable, spread eagle, with her ass, literally, up in the air. Errol gave her a sound slap on the butt then reached for an instrument of some kind on the table.

"What's that?" She tried to sound intrigued rather than fearful, but knew she failed.

He cocked a wicked brow. "A new toy."

The object looked like an eight inch long pear with a sleek and smooth surface. He ran the fat end of the pear between her legs, from her back side up to her navel. Repeatedly, he passed the pear over her increasingly beckoning and moist lips.

"You want to know what it's going to feel like, don't you." Chuckling with deep arousal, Errol eased the pear-like object inside her.

The size of the object scared her and for a moment she tensed up.

"Ease up, Taryn. You're going to love this." He pushed it in deeper. Still holding on the end of the pear, he knelt back and looked down at her. "No matter how I look at you, you're so beautiful," he growled, bending down to lick her wet folds, while moving the wand-like object around, causing different but deep sensations with each angle. Errol was right, this was heavenly. Her nipples puckered tighter, and her entire body clenched in the explosive sensations coming from Errol's mouth, his hands, and the thrusting object in her. She gave an orgasmic cry before shuddering violently with pleasure.

As the last wave of orgasm swept through her, he thrust deep into her, rocking along with her trembles until he came with a loud grunt, calling out "Taryn, my angel," before he collapsed on top of her, kissing her deeply then tenderly against her jawline, her cheeks and her lips. "My sweet girl, that wasn't that bad, wasn't it?" He smiled a boyish sweet smile, happy to have found a new game to play with his playmate. "Let's try it once again, only..." he pushed the pear-like head back into her, wiggled it, and bent his head down to lick her clit. He was devouring her to the point of climax when the lights suddenly went out.

"Errol?" Instant panic swept through Taryn as total blackness engulfed her. "What's going on?"

"Don't worry. It's probably just a fuse or something."

She heard his receding footsteps. "Where are you going?"

"Don't move," he said. "I wouldn't want that thing to get lodged in there."

As he called his warning, the object sank deeper inside her. "Errol, I don't like this." She wanted desperately to release the hold her feet had on the table and lay her legs back on the floor, but she feared the consequences of the strange object inside her.

From a short distance away, she heard him tap his knuckles against the glass of a window. "Looks like the whole neighborhood is out."

"Untie me, Errol. I don't like this. I don't want to do this anymore." Taryn fought against the panic rising within her...the panic she had never told anyone before that she faced...total darkness.

"Relax. It doesn't change anything. You were blindfolded just a minute ago and you didn't panic."

"I know, but this isn't the same. Now you can't see what you're doing, either. Besides, I don't like have this thing..."

"Take it easy, Taryn." His footsteps sounded across the dining room floor and out toward the large storage closet by the front door.

"Don't leave me alone, Errol. Please."

"I'm just going to get a few candles. You know this might turn out to be even better than I'd planned."

Through the darkness she heard him rummage through boxes.

"Hurry."

"Okay, I got them."

Taryn let out a hiss of stressed relief. Though she tried to stay calm, panic refused to stay at bay.

"Now all we need is a lighter or match to..."

A loud thud was followed by the even louder clamor of a dead drop.

"Errol?"

Silence clung to the darkness.

"Errol!" Her loud pants of panic filled the room while the pounding of her heart thundered in her ears. In a brief moment of lucidity amidst her panic, she held her breath and listened for sounds of his breathing.

Nothing. Her panic resumed.

The blackness weighed down on her, collapsing over her and leaving her feeling trapped. Ignoring the possible consequences of moving her legs while the awful gadget was shoved up inside her, she put her legs on the floor and tried to think rationally.

But rational thought escaped her as the need to free herself overpowered her. She struggled against the handcuffs, hoping the table legs would yield. They didn't budge. In her struggles to get loose, she banged her fists against the floor, but noticed, a moment too late, that she'd inadvertently tightened the handcuffs around her wrists.

"Errol!" she shouted into the abyss.

Silence answered her back as she fought desperately against the dark.

Chapter 21

Errol's first waking thoughts centered on the pounding headache that throbbed along the width of his forehead. "What the hell…?" He opened his eyes to the complete blackness that surrounded him, closed them again as he tried to understand what had happened then opened them again.

After a few seconds of staring into nothingness, his memory slowly brought him to the moments just before he'd knocked himself out. Taryn… he'd handcuffed her, or was that just part of the fantasy he'd created?

Sitting up, he held his head in his hands for a long moment. The initial throbbing along his brow had spread to envelope his entire head with a strange numbing sensation. His ears popped and he felt strangely congested. His jaw hurt, the dull jolts of pain driving up to his teeth. He felt as if his brain wanted to seep out of every orifice.

He slowly got to his feet and stretched his hands out in front of him to find the nearest wall.

"Taryn," he softly called out. His voice reverberated in his head and he leaned into the wall for support. "Taryn."

A rage of bile rose to his throat as he remembered where he'd left her... and in what position. "Taryn!" Running his hands over the wall, he tried to imagine where he was. Then he remembered he'd gone to the storage closet for candles.

Leaving the security of the wall, he stooped over and tapped the floor around him until he found the candles. Holding his hands blindly in front of him, he took slow careful steps until he touched the soft leather of his sofa. He followed the back of the sofa to the end table and opened the small drawer hoping to find a lighter. Aside from a pad of paper, a few pens and an old remote control, there was nothing. He went on a few paces until he came to a chair set at the end of his dinner table. Among the objects there, he knew there was a box of long stick matches. Searching with his hands, he finally found it, slipped it open and pulled out a match.

The instant he struck it to a flame, he saw Taryn lying limp under the table, one wrist still handcuffed to the table, while the other…bruised, with the handcuff still on, but free from its chain. Taryn had managed to break the link to free herself. Errol's heart sank.

Immediately dropping to his knees, he caressed her cheek. "Taryn, baby. I'm here Taryn. Everything's going to be all right." He kissed her forehead, her lips, and her wrists. "I'm so sorry, baby. I didn't know. I couldn't get back in time…"

The dry tracks of tears streaked down across her face as she stared blindly up at the underside of the table. Beads of sweat trickled down either side of her forehead and a red welt showed where she'd smashed her head against the floor.

"Taryn," he said as he gently shook her shoulder.

She turned away from him.

"I'm sorry, baby. I was only gone a minute." In truth, he had no idea how long he'd really been out.

"I'm here now." He gulped back tears. "I'm so sorry…"

Taryn couldn't even move at first, she could only rock back and forth, her naked arms around herself, trying to keep from shuddering. Being chained in pitched black…it was her worst nightmare, but one that seemed like a distant memory. Something she couldn't remembered because it happened when she was so young. She couldn't remember; she had no energy for that.

She only knew that her body had a memory, and it was deathly afraid of what went on in pitch black darkness.

And if Chef Errol King was aroused by that, liked playing games in the dark, then she knew what she had to do.

Epilogue

Charles-de-Gaulle airport faded to nothing as the plane took off, leaving Paris far, far behind. Her dreams for the future, her new love, her sexual apprenticeship... all abandoned. Taryn stared out the window as the plane pierced through the clouds that hovered over the city of lights. The sun shined brilliantly against a sky of pure blue.

She would have preferred to remain in the murky grays of the dense clouds.

The decision had been difficult, but in the end, she knew it was the only one she could live with. Errol had shown, beyond her darkest nightmares, how heartless and brutal he could be. He'd proven himself to be worse than the rumors she'd so often heard about him.

"Coffee? Café?" the flight attendant said as he rolled a cart down the aisle. "Brioche?"

She nodded and reached out for a cup. "Café. Merci."

Like a moth to a flame, his gaze landed on the scars on her wrist and he offered her a quick and sympathetic nod.

Taryn concentrated her gaze on her coffee and quickly pulled the cuff of her blouse over the red rings that encircled her wrists; reminders of her struggle against the handcuffs. While her blouse hid a good portion of the marks left on her skin, it didn't manage to hide the scratches and scraped that went halfway up the back of her hands, some of which had turned a nasty shade of blue.

Thankfully, the flight to New York was only half booked. Not only had it allowed her to get a seat at the last minute, but she also had the luxury of having an empty seat beside her. One less person to look quizzically at the scars she bore.

She leaned back against the headrest and looked outside. Why did it have to come to this? she wanted to say to Errol. *Why did you have to push me too far? Why did you leave me there alone to freak out in the dark? It was my first time in handcuffs… you must have known how insecure I already felt about that. Why does loving you have to be filled with so much pain?* Perhaps she should have stayed around and asked him that point blank. Either too cowardly or too shook up by the events of the night before, she'd chosen the easy way out, and had packed her bags and left in the dark of night.

Closing her eyes, she immediately saw his face and a pang of regret tugged at her heart. It was inconceivable. How could she have let herself fall in love with such a man? He was all passion, all consuming, so much more experienced in life and sex than her. He was the kind of man, any woman would lose their minds over. Being with him was like being in the middle of a tornado, safe but wildly dangerous at the same time. One move out of the center, could rip her to shreds.

In love? Could she truly be in love with him? He was a brute, an arrogant know-it-all and a jealous freak all rolled into one. What was there to love?

That boyish grin when they worked together. The joyous gleam in his eyes when he looked at her. The tender touch of his hands all over her body.

Is that enough?

Clearly not, she answered herself.

And your diploma?

"It can wait until later," she muttered.

"Pardon?"

Taryn opened her eyes and looked at the flight attendant who was on his way back with his empty cart. "Sorry. Nothing."

He grinned and continued on.

The flight seemed endless as Taryn tried to find ways to keep her mind occupied. Sleep was out of the question. The moment she closed her eyes, all she could see was Errol, and in the one brief dream she'd slipped into, he was naked and glorious as he reached out to pull her into his arms. She had slept with him almost every night since she had arrived in Paris…how could her body leave his warmth, his touch, the soft kisses, and the fiery passion?

She flipped through a few magazines, but nothing interested her. Even a popular cooking magazine with recipes that might have otherwise interested her could not hold her attention. She looked out the window… same clear blue sky, only the sun was in a different place.

A sigh escaped her as she tried to imagine the conversation she would have with her mother once she got home. Only an hour remained before the cityscape she knew so well came into view.

Her mother would be furious. And how could Taryn explain it? She had no idea.

The seatbelt light came on, and soon JFK came into view. Taryn took the soft and gentle landing as a good omen. She took her bag out of the overhead compartment and breathed a strangled sigh of relief as she left the plane.

She was on her home turf now… safe, secure… predictable.

Before she reached the end of the terminal, she turned her phone on to call her mother. Instead, her phone beeped out its signal of an oncoming text message.

Her hand shook. It had to be him, but did she want to know what he said? There was nothing he could say; nothing he could do. It was over.

She stopped walking and stood there while passengers filed left and right of her. A few grumbled and groaned, but only when a large New Yorker with an attitude demanded she move aside did she realize where she was. Muttering an apology, she walked out of the terminal and harbored in a quiet corner.

After a moment of hesitation, she checked her phone to see there were seven texts. She'd just barely boarded the plane when Errol had sent the first one.

Where are you?

It was so typical of him. She was distraught and confused and he was just angry to see she wasn't there where she was supposed to be. Five minutes later, he sent the next text.

I see you've packed your things. Did you go off with that Henri kid? You know how I feel about that. Are you trying to run me off a cliff with jealousy?

"Way to go, Errol. Just keep digging yourself in deeper," Taryn muttered. The next text was sent fifteen minutes later.

Just talked to Henri and he said he has no idea where you are. Where are you?

Two minutes.

I know last night was difficult for you. Believe me, I never intended to traumatize you. If you left because of that, you have to come back. Let me make

269

it up to you. You know I'd never hurt you. Taryn, please.

Thirty seconds.

Answer me, Taryn!

Ten seconds.

Sorry, Taryn. I just can't believe you're gone. Are you heading back home? Go to New York? How could you do that? And leave everything behind? Me? Your diploma? What are you thinking, Taryn? Please, just let me know where you are. Let me know you're okay. I never meant to hurt you. Please see me.

One minute.

Taryn, I know you aren't answering my texts, but know this. The last couple of months with you have changed me, challenged me in many ways, taken me to places emotionally and physically that I never thought I could go. I never thought I could have such a strong instant connection to you, to anyone, but when I read your desire to attend The Institute, then saw your photo; it reached into me and pulled at me until I had to take a chance with you. I'm scared about us, just as you are. I don't think I could ever feel this way about anyone...please, Taryn...come back to me.

Kailin Gow

*****

Taryn and Errol's story continues in:

Savor Me (Volume 2, Master Chefs Series)

A Sneak Peak at:

Savor Me

Master Chefs #2

Kailin Gow

Prologue

"Over here, Miss Taryn Cummings."

Caught in the busy come and go of JFK airport, Taryn turned to see her brother in the crowd, waving her over. He flashed her a mocking grin. Forcing a smile, she waved and maneuvered her way to him. "Bobby," she said as she gave him a hug. "What are you doing here? Mom made you come out and get me, huh?"

He kissed her cheek and took her suitcase. "Hey, what an opinion you have of your little brother. I offered to come."

"Yeah, I know how you love to drive through traffic, wrestle into a parking space and elbow your way through this crowd... all to come and help me lug my suitcase back out... How far are you parked?"

Chuckling, he put his arm around her shoulder and escorted her out. "It's a beautiful day for a walk in the Big A. I'm sure after being cooped up in that plane for hours, a little fresh air will do you good."

Shielding his eyes from the blinding sun, he stopped and looked out at the field of cars. "Now, if only I could remember where I left that big, black sucker."

Taryn looked at him. "Mom let you take her Lexus?"

"Hey, I'm offended. You say that like I'm not trustworthy." He continued to scan the parking lot.

"Seriously, Bobby. Where d'you park it?"

He nudged her playfully with his elbow and turned to the left. Sooner than he'd let on, they arrived at the large SUV. After tossing her suitcase into the back seat, they got in and drove off.

"So?"

"So?"

"How's my driving?"

"Your driving? I just came home from months in France and you want me to comment on your driving?"

"Ever since you got in the car, you've been checking my blind spot, looking behind us, making sure I make a full stop. Relax, *ma grande soeur*, I know how to drive."

"And you've been learning a bit of French, too?"

"Well, you've been there so long, I thought maybe you wouldn't understand English anymore." He laughed at himself.

"You're such a silly goof."

"Ha, that's not what Kristy said last night."

Taryn leaned her head back into the headrest. "Please, spare me the details of your torrid love life."

"It's not torrid. It's just busy."

She turned to look at him. "I must admit, *mon petit frere*, you do look good." She reached out to finger a blond lock that lightly brushed against the nape of his neck. "You let your hair grow in a bit."

"Yeah... the girls love it."

Taryn laughed. "I imagine they would. So, besides staying busy with the ladies, what you been up to?"

"Still taking those cooking classes at college. You know, girls love that, too. Do you know how much girls are turned on by a guy who knows how to cook?"

"Yeah," Taryn droned. "Tell me about it."

"And at my age. I mean, girls don't expect a good looking, eighteen year old guy to be so talented in the kitchen... you know what I mean?"

"You're an eternal flirt, you know that?"

"Yep."

"And so humble."

"I do what I can. Besides, false humility never did anybody good."

Taryn snorted. "What about the restaurant?"

"Busy. I'm there more than thirty hours a week now."

"Thirty? And when do you go to college?"

"Pretty much the rest of the time. I have to admit, between running the kitchen and keeping my grades up, I don't have much time to fool around."

Taryn grinned and affectionately patted his hand. "I'm sure you manage to find time."

Glancing at her, he flashed her his killer smile.

No wonder the girls all fall for him, she thought. *He is pretty darn cute.*

"You know, now that you've dropped all this Paris business, why don't you take a course with me at college."

"I don't think so. I'm going to concentrate on giving mom a hand at the restaurant. The hours I put in will give you a break."

"Ah, come on. It'd be fun. I mean, I know it's not a Parisian institute or nothing, but it's a decent course. I've already learned a lot. And not just about cooking. I'm taking a restaurant management course now."

"Thanks, Bobby, but I honestly can't imagine working with you most of the day then going off to take the same classes as you. I think a sibling relationship can only take so much togetherness."

Looking straight ahead, he snorted. "Yeah, I think you're right."

As they drove in front of La Benicoise, one of the restaurants Errol had opened in New York, Taryn's heart skipped a beat. She'd managed to put him out of her mind the entire twenty minutes she'd spent catching up with Bobby, but now the thought of him struck her unexpectedly and knocked the air out of her.

Savor Me continues Taryn and Errol's story. Sold at every e-retailer.

Get a Free Full-length Book when you subscribe to Kailin's newsletter!

https://dl.bookfunnel.com/5rmis5rrj1

www.ingramcontent.com/pod-product-compliance
Lightning Source LLC
Chambersburg PA
CBHW052035240626

47153CB00006B/2095